The Masters Review

ten stories

The Masters Review

The Masters Review Volume VI
Stories Selected by Roxane Gay
Edited by Kim Winternheimer and Sadye Teiser

Front cover: Adobe Stock 102053695
Design by Kim Winternheimer

Interior design by Kim Winternheimer

First printing.

ISBN: 978-0-9853407-5-9

Printed in the USA

The Masters Review

ten stories

Volume VI

Gabriel Moseley · Amy Purcell · Leslie Jones
Matthew Sullivan · Kasey Thornton
Chris Arp · Rachel Engelman · Michele Host
Maria Thomas · Nicole Cuffy

Stories Selected by Roxane Gay
Edited by Kim Winternheimer and Sadye Teiser

Editor's Note

This is the fourth volume of *The Masters Review* that I have had the privilege to work on with Founding Editor Kim Winternheimer. Every year, we publish stories by ten emerging writers. And, each year, I am blown away by the strength and variety of the pieces we publish. I am proud to be an editor of a publication that offers a level playing field to writers who are early in their careers. As the number of stories we receive continues to grow, our deliberations become all the more difficult.

This year, we had the honor of working with guest judge Roxane Gay. Roxane has established herself as an incisive voice in fiction and nonfiction, as a talented editor, and as one of our most respected cultural critics. She is the author of the essay collection *Bad Feminist*, the novel *An Untamed State*, the story collection *Difficult Women,* and the memoir *Hunger*. She teaches at Purdue University and is a contributing opinion writer for *The New York Times*. Roxane's work is bold, nuanced, and vital, and I was right to expect nothing less of the stories she selected.

Stories are vehicles of great political and social force, both as records of and as catalysts for change. In compliment—not contradiction—to a story's political power is its timelessness. All good stories speak to a seed of humanity within the reader; they elicit an emotion that is free from time. They work from the inside out. These ten tales are powerful examples of this phenomenon.

The stories in this collection span many disparate places, times, and perspectives. We hear from a teenage boy in the Britain of 1837 who is fascinated by the taboo nature of a romantic attraction between two men. In another story, a father tries to teach his son to stand up for himself against the backdrop of a reality television show in which families live in the wilderness, in cabins without modern conveniences. In a fairy tale world at once familiar and new, a lady-in-waiting recounts her romance with the Queen. We accompany a woman as she discovers a man who is little enough to fit into her Lucky Strikes tin. At the same time, the woman struggles to come to terms with her own son's violent nature.

In all these stories—about characters different from ourselves in circumstances so different than our own—we find a glimmer of humanity we recognize. No other anthology that I have edited encapsulates such a wide range of histories and voices, and this is what sets our sixth volume apart. The variety of stories here is what makes this such a special collection.

In a way, I really think I have the easiest job in the world, helping to select and edit these pieces. The stories in this collection all stood out for their technical merits: they are well constructed on the sentence level, expertly plotted, sublimely readable. But they also hook the reader in a way that is felt before you can explain it. They hit on something timeless and visceral.

Authors from past anthologies have gone on to do great things, and I am sure that this year's group is no exception. *The Masters Review* authors have found agents, put out their first books, and published in distinguished literary journals throughout the country. Our third volume won the Silver Medal INDIEFAB Book Award for Best Short Story Collection by an Independent Press, and we are happy to have received a fellowship from Oregon Literary Arts. We are proud to continue our tradition of introducing distinct and powerful new voices in contemporary fiction.

Please join me in welcoming these ten authors to the literary landscape. We can't wait to see what they do next.

—Sadye Teiser
Editorial Director

Contents

Introduction

When I am judging a literary contest, I am often asked what I am looking for in a good short story or essay. I offer up the kinds of work I am not really interested in reading—stories about college students, stories about writers, stories about sad white people in sad marriages, stories about addiction, stories about cancer. This probably seems overly prescriptive but when you read a certain kind of story too many times, you develop emotional callouses. The only thing that heals those emotional callouses is great writing that offers up something refreshing and unexpected, whether it's a writing style or a unique character or a rich sense of place or an unforgettable plot.

I am looking for writing that I will continue thinking about long after I have finished reading, for writing I want to read over and over again, for writing that will always stay with me. As I read the stories and essays for *The Master's Review Volume VI*, I took my time. I read most of them while on book tour, on airplanes, and the stories I loved most were those that made me forget that I was in the middle of an exhausting tour on yet another terrible flight.

In "A Man Stands Tall," I loved the premise, of a family doing one of those reality competitions where people pretend to live in a different time, without the comforts of modernity. The writing was crisp and precise and as the story proceeded, I kept wondering how it would all end, and then when I got to the end, I lost my breath, literally. I gasped, staring at the page, unsure of what I had just read and so I re-read it to see if I had misunderstood. I had not. And the audacity of the ending, the fierceness of it, made me put the stack of stories and essays down and just stare out the window and the clouds. A few minutes later I read the story again, and again and my goodness, my appreciation for the work only grew. If I could put into words how that story has made me feel since I first read it, that is what I would say every time I am asked what I am looking for.

The ten stories I selected for this anthology all moved me in that same way, where I either gasped or my heart pounded or my mind was simply blown by the story the writer had created. Take "Gormley," for example. This is not the kind of story I am typically drawn to but the writing was delicate and careful and so perfectly matched to the setting. I was immersed in the world of the story and did not want to emerge from it. I felt the same way about "Confessions of a Lady-In-Waiting," the title of which becomes doubly brilliant when you get to the end of the story. There was such an unexpected turn of events just past the middle of the story, and throughout, so much lush detail about the royal court, the king and queen, the women who served them in all ways.

"Migrations," about a social service worker who is looking in on a family whose children have not been seen out of their home in quite some time, is haunting and a sly, sly commentary on race in America. "Little Men," was one of the strangest stories I have ever read. I am still unsettled by the little man in the story and the woman who carries him around and the life she is living and how what seems like an odd domestic story is actually so much more.

And though I rarely am interested in stories about sad white people in sad marriages, there was one such story that absolutely made me forget I ever said I was not interested in such stories. In "Speakers of Other Languages," a long married couple finds their long, unspoken arrangement quietly shattered when a member of the construction crew, working on their home renovation, becomes the source of great interest.

The other stories I selected were equally compelling to me. "Out of Our Suffering" is exactly the kind of story I love so my bar is high. This story exceeded that bar and then some because it was so unflinching and full of heart. I marveled at the plainspoken but powerful narrative voice of "Steal Away," a story about sharecroppers not so long after slavery's end. An Alaskan man trying to make sense of his responsibility toward his family is at the center of "Hope Gold," and a sister also grapples with such responsibility as she tries her best to love and look after her bipolar brother in "This Is an Exercise in Detachment."

I read thirty stories for this anthology and it was very difficult to narrow down that list to only ten. There are no more emotional callouses here. To read writing of the caliber of stories I was lucky enough to read is one of many reminders that this is a remarkable time to be alive and reading. I hope, as you read these ten stories, that you feel the same.

—Roxane Gay

The Masters Review

ten stories

A Man Stands Tall

Gabriel Moseley

I.

By the time the boy neared home, the sun was already sinking toward the snow-dusted ridge of the Bitterroot Mountains. He walked through the meadow slowly, cradling his right hand with his left. The cameraman, dressed all in black, followed the boy like a distant shadow—always present, but unobtrusive. The sound of wood chopping echoed through the valley. When he got closer to the log cabin, the boy paused. He rubbed away the last trace of tears from his eyes and slid his injured hand beneath his sleeve.

As the boy approached, Tom raised and swung his axe in one smooth motion, splitting the log below into two even chunks. The boy stood there, waiting, but Tom said nothing. He set another log on the chopping block, without looking at his son. He had already chopped more than enough wood for the day, but he wanted to teach his son a lesson.

"Sorry I'm late," Ajay said.

"Sorry doesn't chop wood."

The cameraman circled around them with soft, measured steps, adjusting the angle of his shot. They did not pay attention to his movements. After three months of being on the show, of living under near constant observation, they had gotten better at pretending that the cameramen were no more remarkable than dirt.

"I'll chop twice my share tomorrow," Ajay said, keeping his arm behind him.

"Where were you?"

"Playing in the foothills. We lost track of time."

"Don't let it happen again," Tom said. He lifted the axe over his shoulder, resting the wooden haft against his neck. "You understand me?"

Ajay nodded.

"Good. Go help your mother with dinner."

As his son climbed up the steps to their log cabin, Tom's expression softened. One of the main reasons he'd wanted to be on *Homesteaders* in the first place was to toughen up his son. The idea of the show was simple: three modern families uproot and live for six months like genuine Montana pioneers. No competition, no reality show scripted fakery, no one-on-one confessions to the cameras—just well-documented rustic living. And it was already doing his son good. Instead of staring at screens all day, his son, his chubby, fourteen-year-old, videogame-addicted son, was now exploring the wilderness, with real friends. The Duke boys were polite and they were athletes—they were not digital avatars. Not zeros and ones. Thanks to the show, Ajay's face was already less soft, his arms less bat-winged, his skin a darker shade of pale.

Tom heaved the axe, pulling force from deep in his legs. He felt the intense yet simple pleasure of the thing as the log cracked apart and the bit of the blade sank deep into the chopping block. At a physical level, it was better than anything from his normal line of work, selling Audis. This was different—something he felt with his bones. With his newly calloused hands. He stared out at the horizon, at the humbling immensity of the distant mountains, and he listened. He listened to the steady hum of crickets, to the quiet rush of the stream cutting through the woods behind his cabin. He could already smell the rabbit stew being cooked inside. Rabbits he had trapped and skinned himself. Vegetables he had grown on his own land.

II.

When he got back inside the cabin, Helen was kneeling in front of their son, examining his broken finger. The pinky, snapped at its base, stuck outward from his hand, the flesh swollen and blue.

"What the hell?" Tom said.

"I fell."

"Ouch," Tom said. "Why didn't you say something?"

Before Ajay could answer, Helen hugged the boy against her chest. She brushed her hand through his curly hair, petting the back of his head. Tom started toward them, then stopped.

She hugged Ajay tighter, pressing her cheek to his. To Tom, her features had always seemed suited to sorrow. Her cheekbones, her eyes, her slender strength, all gave her a particular kind of beauty. A melancholy grace. Her long blonde hair had paled from the long hours under the sun.

The cameraman stooped down beside her, aiming the camera to get a better close up of the tender moment. Breaking the show's rules, Helen sneered, staring directly at the cameraman in disgust. She rose to her feet, purposefully blocking the cameraman's view, and walked to the makeshift kitchen, where she pulled out a jug of moonshine whiskey. She poured a trickle into a mason jar and then stirred in a long pour of honey with a spoon. When she offered it to Ajay, he drank it down, choking a little at the whiskey's fire.

"This is what it takes for you guys to let me drink?" he said, smiling sadly. He held up his pinky for them both to see.

"That's the spirit," Tom said, laughing. He patted Ajay on the back. "Nothing a little white lightning can't cure."

"Very funny," she said. "We need to get it checked out by a doctor."

Tom examined the pinky more closely, touching it gently. Ajay winced.

"I think he'll be okay," Tom said. "I bet we can fix it."

"Oh, you bet?" she said. "What if you're wrong?"

The cameraman backed away quietly into the corner of the cabin, establishing a more panoramic view. Helen stepped in front of him and tapped her finger against the eye of the lens.

"Can you leave us alone for one fucking minute?"

The cameramen said nothing. He kept filming.

"Come on, he's just doing his job," Tom said. "We should fix this ourselves. That's the whole point of the show."

"Bullshit," she said.

They argued. They argued about the rules of the show and what counted as an emergency—what was worth breaking the rules over and what was not. They argued about how thorough the show's brief medical training session had been, and then whether the original Montana homesteaders would or would not have made use of a modern doctor, if one had been available. Then they argued about who was trying to argue and who was not. While they argued, Ajay stared at his broken finger, then down at the floor.

Finally, exhausted, Helen let Tom have his way. He whittled down two splint sticks out of kindling and she found the cloth bolt and a cord of twine. She ripped off a length of cloth with quiet fury.

When they forced the finger back straight, Ajay cried silently, shuddering at the pain. They sandwiched his finger between the splint sticks, set it tightly against the buddy finger with cloth, and then wrapped it all together. Helen hugged Ajay again.

"It's okay, Sweetie," she said. "It's over."

It might not have been perfect, Tom thought, but at least they had fixed it on their own. Back home, they would have rushed Ajay to the hospital, waited an hour, and paid a doctor an arm and a leg to tell them, in Latin, that his son had broken his pinky. And the doctor would have done the exact same thing, except with gauze and tape and metal.

Although Tom tried to ignore the cameras, he couldn't help but think of all the families that were watching them. In his mind's eye, he pictured their little domestic drama multiplied on screens across America, across the world. All those families would be watching them, their faces lit up by the flickering light of their TVs, marveling at how far he and his family had come, how self-reliant they now were, after only a few months of simulated frontier living. He pictured the images of himself, replicating endlessly.

"You did great," Tom said to Ajay, patting his head. "Very brave."

He approached his wife from behind and laid his hands on her shoulders, feeling the smoothness of the thin fabric of her dress, as he began to lightly massage the knots from her shoulders. "You must admit," he said, "we did pretty good." She shrugged away from him. She pulled the steaming copper pot of stew off of the woodstove and set it down hard on the table.

III.

Late that night, Tom awoke to find that Helen was not in bed. The room was dark. He drew the warm blanket up around him against the cold. Because the cabin was only one big room, they had set up a curtain to separate it into two private sleeping areas. Ajay snored gently from beyond the other side of the curtain.

When Helen did not return after several minutes, Tom got out of bed. He pulled his jacket over his bare skin and made his way through the cabin, careful not to wake his son. He smelled the pipe tobacco before he saw her. He peered out the window and watched her taking puffs from the corncob pipe, her blonde hair ghostly white in the light of the low hanging moon.

When he joined her on the porch, neither of them spoke. He sank into the rocking chair next to hers, pulling his jacket tighter around him, scrunching his bare toes. She stared out over the meadow. The fog had rolled down from the mountains to settle in the valley, where it drifted through the black stalks of grass.

"Sorry about before," he said.

"Yeah," she said, placing a hand on his knee. "Sorry I scared the cameraman."

"He was terrified," he said, laughing gently.

"Maybe he won't come back."

"Yeah," he said. "At least they don't watch us sleep, right?"

"Small mercy," she said quietly.

After taking another puff, she passed him the pipe. He took a few deep, slow inhales of the sweet, aromatic smoke and the embers in the bowl crackled and glowed with each draw of breath. It reminded him of when they were first dating, when they'd smoke cigarettes on the fire escape of her apartment in Los Feliz, even though neither of them really smoked. The way they would sit and talk and stare out at the lights of the restless city. It was their ritual. A thing they did when they were young and their love was simple.

"I'm worried about Ajay," she said.

"He'll be fine. We fixed it the same as any doctor."

"That's not what I mean," she said, turning toward him. "Do you really think he broke it falling?"

"That's what he said."

"It doesn't feel right. I think they did this to him," she said. "Those brothers."

"Wouldn't he tell us?"

She hesitated, looking into his eyes, as if she were weighing him in some way.

"He doesn't want you to think he's weak."

They'd argued about this kind of thing before. They had different ideas on how to help Ajay become the person he wanted to become. They'd even argued about the Duke brothers, when Ajay would come home scraped up—whether they played too rough, or were just boys being boys. But there had been problems with bullying before. Never anything that physical, that they knew of, but there had been bullying at his middle school—spit on his shirt, a stolen favorite hat, fat jokes scrawled across his locker.

He didn't want to believe it. He liked the boys. He'd never seen them complain about anything, even though their mom had died from Leukemia a few years before. He'd encouraged Ajay to become friends with them.

"I'll talk to Ajay tomorrow," he said. "And if you're right, I'll put an end to it. I promise."

On the mountains beyond, the moon lit up the white of the snow and the distant stands of trees cast long black shadows. The sky was cloudless, the stars bright. Except for the steady flowing of the unseen stream, all was quiet and still.

IV.

In the morning, after all their chores were done, Tom took his son fishing. They gathered up their fly fishing gear—all 1885 Homesteader appropriate—and they set out, following along the shady path of the stream to the river. One cameraman stayed behind at the cabin to watch Helen and the other cameraman followed them along the stream, keeping a respectful distance. On the way to the river, they passed a point where they could see the Dukes' cabin, on the other side of the stream. The Dukes' cabin was a little nicer than theirs—it was bigger, the raw wood was painted, and it had multiple rooms. Smoke poured from the chimney. But no one was outside. Tom watched Ajay closely as they passed by, but his son said nothing.

When they got to their favorite spot, they cast their fishing lines out into the wide, fast-flowing river, the lines snaking elegantly in the air, as if in slow motion. The day was sunny, the air crisp. The trout liked to rest in the deeper pools on the other side of the river, lying near the bottom, so they aimed for the far side. The cameraman, wearing Converse high tops, stepped carefully out into the river, wading up to his thighs to get a better shot.

After standing in the icy river for nearly an hour, Ajay got a bite. Tom helped him reel it in, showing him, once again, how to release tension before pulling it in farther, to better exhaust the fish. When Ajay pulled it into the shallows, Tom netted the silvery trout, pulled it out by its wriggling tail, and bashed its head against a rock with a wet slap.

It was only later in the afternoon, after they had caught and gutted a few more fish that Tom started to ask about what had really happened to the pinky. They were lying next to each other, resting in the shade of a tree, their bare feet drying in the grass, when he said that Ajay could, and should, always feel free to tell his parents anything—anything at all. "I know," Ajay said. Trying a different tactic, Tom asked him how, exactly, he had fallen. Ajay told him he tripped. But when he answered, Tom noticed that Ajay kept glancing toward the camera watching them.

"Hey," Tom said to the cameraman. "You mind giving us a few minutes?"

The cameraman kept filming.

"Come on, man," Tom said.

The cameraman lowered his camera, shaking his head. "You guys can't keep breaking the rules," he said.

"Just give us a minute."

The cameraman shook his head as he walked away, muttering something about how the producer was going to flip his shit. They watched him walk back upstream, stumbling slightly on the rocks.

"So what happened?" Tom said.

Ajay twirled the fishhook between his fingers. He looped the fishing line around his index finger, until the tip of the finger whitened.

"We were just messing around. Throwing rocks and stuff. Then Brandon asked if I wanted to join their club. They call themselves the Apaches."

"And?"

"He said that to join I had to kill one of the Atkinson's chickens. He said that nobody would ever know I did it. He told me they both killed one and just made it look like the coyotes got them. I said I wouldn't do it and they got mad. Brandon made me pinky swear that I wouldn't tell anyone what they'd done. But when I reached out my pinky, he grabbed it and he—he twisted until it snapped."

"Jesus," Tom said.

"He said he didn't mean to break it. He said sorry."

"Jesus," he said again. "That doesn't matter, Ajay. You can't let people treat you like that."

"I know, I just…" Ajay's voice trailed off and he looked back up the river. "I'm sorry."

"No, you did nothing wrong," Tom said. "You did good. You stuck up for what was right." When he wrapped his arm around his son's shoulder, Ajay sobbed into his little hands.

When he thought about telling Helen, Tom could picture how it all would go. She'd want to talk it out with the boys, talk it out with their father, talk it out with everyone—maybe even the film crew. She'd want to hear everyone's side to the story and then come to some diplomatic solution—the brothers would be punished by having a time out and writing an essay about what they had done wrong, or some similar bullshit. And what good would it do?

They had only found out about the bullying after Tom saw Ajay killing the baby sparrows in the back yard. Ajay didn't know anyone was watching. He was just standing there, staring at the fallen nest, and then he started stomping, over and over, crushing the nest flat. Tom knew it had been a cry for help, but still. The image haunted him. It was only then that Ajay told him about the bullying—the grief and shame he'd been choking back for months.

Tom had wanted to teach Ajay to stand up for himself, like his father had taught him—if someone hits you, hit him back twice as hard. But no. Helen had insisted that Ajay should tell on the bullies so they could sit down with everyone involved. They'd all met in the principal's office. The bullies formally apologized, they were suspended for a week, and they had to write essays about how bullying was wrong—but this only humiliated Ajay further. Helen meant well, but she knew nothing of this world—boys will never respect a boy that has his mother fight his battles for him.

If they talked it out with the Dukes, Tom could see a repeat of that whole thing. Dave would tell them that his boys were acting out because of the loss of their mother, which was no doubt true. Leukemia was a brutal way to die. But all bullies have sob stories. And Ajay would learn, once again, that instead of dealing with his problems on his own he should go running to Mommy.

As he watched the sun flickering on the surface of the river, Tom felt that this was one of those moments where someone's life could fork. He could either teach his son how to be scared for the rest of his life, how to be a coward, or he could finally teach his son how a man stands tall.

"We'll fix this," he said.

Ajay looked up, his eyes red, and wiped his snotty nose on his forearm. "How?"

Without saying a word, Tom grabbed one of his socks and walked to the river. He scooped up a handful of smooth, wet river stones and poured them into the mouth of the sock. He hefted the sock, testing its weight, and then added a few more stones. He walked back and handed the sock mace to his wide-eyed son.

"Do you know the story of David and Goliath?" he asked.

"Yeah."

"You don't have to be bigger or stronger than your enemy,"

he said. "You just have to be smarter."

Ajay stared at the sock mace like it was a grenade.

"Don't use this unless it is absolutely necessary," Tom said. "I mean it. Always try to talk it out. If they call you names, you ignore them. You walk away. Be the bigger man. Always avoid a fight if you possibly can. But if they try to hurt you again, I want you to use that. And use it like you mean it."

"Ok, Dad," he said.

"And don't show it to anyone. Not even Mom. This is our secret."

Ajay climbed to his feet and started swinging the sock mace, first in a tight, twirling circle around his wrist, then in longer, arcing loops that wooshed through the air, swinging the weapon with his whole arm, slashing down imaginary enemies.

V.

When asked, Tom never lied outright about their talk at the river, he just retold what was said in a way that his wife would understand. He said that the little bastards had been teasing him, it was true, but that the broken finger was an accident—he just tripped when they were chasing him. He told Helen that they talked about ways to stand up for himself, to never let people bully him again, to tell his parents if they tried, that it was always perfectly all right just to walk away. And at first, everything seemed fixed.

Ajay stopped hanging out with the Duke brothers completely. On the day after their talk, Tom was working in the garden when the two of them came over, asking if Ajay wanted to come play. His son walked out and told them, firmly, that he did not want to hangout with them anymore. That he needed to focus on his chores. The brothers had laughed at him, but he didn't back down.

After that, Ajay began to work harder at his tasks. He became less withdrawn, less afraid—it was as if his secret weapon, although unused, let him access an untapped power inside himself.

In the weeks that followed, he even made friends with Claire, the daughter of the Atkinson family. She was quiet and, admittedly, not exactly a looker, but the two took long walks together and, from what Tom saw, they seemed relaxed and satisfied in sharing one another's silence. He even caught them holding hands. And as Ajay seemed more and more content, the tensions eased between him and Helen. They argued less and less. On the few nights that they were not too exhausted from their long days, and only when they were sure Ajay was fast asleep, they quietly made love.

VI.

When Ajay did not come home for dinner, Helen shouted out his name from the porch, again and again, but there was no reply. They had checked all his usual playing spots around the cabin—the place where the stream pools, the boulders on the far side of the meadow. He was not there. The sun dropped behind the mountains, its afterglow staining the clouds red.

Helen was annoyed. It was not like Ajay to be this disrespectful. A little late, fine, she said, but dinner was getting cold. Tom, hyperconscious of the cameras watching him, said that they really needed to teach that kid some goddamn punctuality. Then he forced a cheerful tone, joking about how maybe Ajay finally kissed Claire and liked it so much he couldn't stop.

After they waited as long as they could wait, after the sky was blue and darkening fast, they split up to look for him. Helen went to the Atkinson's, where they both agreed he probably was, and Tom went to look for him at the Dukes' cabin, just in case. The two cameramen followed them silently as they went their separate ways.

As he approached the Duke's cabin, Tom paused. Warm light poured from the windows and, from inside, he caught muffled domestic sounds—the clink and clatter of silverware, soft voices. He calmed his breathing. Nothing was wrong. There was no point in worrying until there was something to worry about. He would ask about Ajay, they'd say he wasn't there, he'd go home, and Ajay would be sitting there at their table, sorry for being late, but safe and sound.

He walked up the steps of their porch and knocked three

times. Dave opened the door. He was small and mousy, but always positive, even if it was forced. A doormat kind of guy.

The cameraman filming the Dukes turned his camera on Tom. The cameraman who had been following Tom stayed outside, to avoid them filming each other. Dave asked if Tom would like to care to come inside and sit a spell. To get in the spirit of the original homesteaders, Dave had started faking a Southern accent.

"No, no, that's okay," Tom said. "I was just hoping you could help me out."

"Of course," Dave said. "Whatcha need, partner?"

Tom was about to explain the situation when he saw Brandon, seated at the table. He had a big, purple bruise swelling over his left eye socket—swollen to the point that it made him look like he was squinting. He had a dirty white sock pulled over his hand. When Brandon caught Tom looking at him, he grinned, waving hello with the sock puppet.

"Well?" Dave said, dropping the accent. "Is everything all right?"

"Yeah," he said, "Sure. I was just—I'm looking for Ajay."

"Ajay?" Dave said. "No, haven't seen him. Have you boys?"

"Nope," John said. "Haven't seen him."

"Me either," Brandon said.

Tom looked around the cabin. Even though their cabin was bigger than his, it didn't seem as nice on the inside. Their cabin was bare. Helen had made their own cabin feel like a real home, with pine branches on the windowsills, with makeshift curtains and rugs, with Ajay's drawings on the walls.

"It's probably nothing," Tom said. "He's probably over at the Atkinson's place. They've been hanging out a lot these days."

"Sure," Dave said. "But if he doesn't turn up, you let me know. I'd be happy to help you look."

Brandon waited until his father turned around, until the camera was pointed away from him, and then raised his sock puppet hand, twisting it left and right, in convincing mimicry of someone searching for something—looking under the table, looking out the window, looking left and right.

"We'd *all* be happy to help you," Brandon said, opening and closing the mouth of the puppet, miming along with his words.

VII.

As Helen argued with the cameraman, Tom paced across the cabin, back and forth, over and over. He barely listened to them. He did not speak.

Finally Helen convinced the man to call his producer.

"Hey, yeah, I guess one of the kids is missing," the cameraman said into the phone. It was the one with the converse high tops. "No, I don't know, no one was with him. I—"

Helen snatched the phone. "You listen to me," she said. "No one's seen my son in hours. I want you to call the police."

Tom slumped down at the table and put his head between his hands.

The image of Brandon and the sock puppet played in his head like a fever dream. He felt crazy, like he had imagined it. But it was real. And he had been too much of a coward to confront the kid then and there. What could he have said? That Brandon must know something, because of a sock puppet? They'd think he was insane. The camera was watching him. He'd thought of the audience, all those eyes. He had done nothing. He'd nursed his pride, instead of helping his son. He dropped his forehead against the table, half-listening to Helen shout into the phone.

With his head still against the table, Tom stared out the window at the blackness of night. Even with glare from the lantern light, he could make out the dark skyline of the mountains. What he had once seen as pretty scenery, he now saw in its true, sovereign form. This was one of the most untamed parts of Montana. There were black bears and grizzlies out there. There were cougars and wolves. The reality of the savageness of his surroundings sank into him like a blade.

"Ask how long they'll take to get here," he said.

She asked, listened to the response, and told him the nearest police station was at least a three-hour drive.

In his mind's eye he tried to picture the vastness of the landscape surrounding him, spreading outwards in all directions. He felt unspeakably small.

Even when they finally got here, the police would have no idea where to look. They knew nothing about what he knew. They would be useless.

He stood up from the table, pulled on his jacket, and headed for the door.

"What are you doing?" Helen said. "They said we should wait for the police."

"I'm going to find him."

As he turned to leave, the cameraman picked up the camera and started filming. When Tom opened the door, the cameraman began to follow him, in quiet, measured steps.

"Don't fucking follow me," Tom snapped. "I'm serious."

When the cameraman kept filming, Tom wrestled the camera out of the man's hands and threw it down to the floor. Then, with one last look at Helen, he headed out into the dark.

VIII.

Tom approached the Duke's cabin and looked for a spot where he could watch the front door while still remaining hidden. He crawled into a thicket of bushes, wriggling through scratchy underbrush on his belly. The glow from the cabin oozed through the windows. The moon was bright.

Within minutes, the front door opened and the cameraman walked outside, talking loudly on his phone. Tom ducked his head down instinctually, but the cameraman couldn't see a thing.

Tom waited under the bushes, cramped in darkness, for what felt like hours. Worst-case nightmare scenarios ran through his head, image after image, unstoppable. Ajay crying, lost in the woods. Ajay lying broken and bleeding at the bottom of a ravine. Wolves stalking closer, drawn by blood.

The front door opened and Brandon walked outside toward their outhouse. There was a little smile on his face, despite the huge bruise, despite the squinty eye. He whistled to himself as he walked.

As soon as Brandon entered the outhouse and shut the door behind him, Tom slipped off his boots and socks. He stalked toward the outhouse, quickly and quietly, stepping carefully between the twigs and branches, crouching low as he passed through the light from the windows. He eased up against the far side of the outhouse, flattened his body against the wall, and waited, his heart hammering inside his chest.

The door creaked open. As Brandon stepped outside, still adjusting his belt, Tom grabbed him from behind. He swiped his arm around his neck and squeezed. Brandon flailed, trying to punch behind him, but Tom caught his thin wrist and twisted the arm behind his back. When he struggled again, Tom wrenched the arm upward.

"Stop," he hissed, "Or I'll break your fucking arm."

He led the boy away from the house, as quietly as he could, walking backward, feeling out the ground with the soles of his feet, glancing behind him to see where he was going, checking back on the house to make sure no one was following. When they were far enough away, he turned the boy around and forced him to walk before him, still gripping the boy's arm. He led him down the riverbank into the rocky shallows.

"Tell me where he is," he said.

Brandon said nothing.

"Tell me," he said. "I'll let you go if you tell me now."

The boy glanced down and stomped his boot onto Tom's bare toes. Pain tore through Tom's foot and his grip slipped. The boy pulled himself away and ran. Tom chased him, sloshing through the water, each step agony on the sharp rocks. He reached out and grabbed the boy's the collar, yanking it, and the boy lurched backward, splashing into the water. When he tried to scramble back to his feet, Tom slapped him across the face as hard as he could. The boy crumpled to his hands and knees.

"Where is he?" he said.

Brandon rose to his knees, staring up at him. He spat at Tom's face.

Tom slapped him again, hard. When the boy clasped his hands to his bleeding nose, Tom grabbed his hair with both hands and pulled him farther into the river. When the river was deep enough, he drove Brandon's head under the freezing water. Tom lifted him back up, Brandon gasped, choking for air, but before he could fill his lungs, Tom forced him under again, holding him down until he thrashed and gurgled.

IX.

Brandon walked in front, his hands tied tight behind his back with Tom's knotted belt. The boy was crying, his bony shoulders convulsing with each sob. Tom did not listen. He gripped the tail end of the belt like he was walking a dog, yanking every now and then to bring the boy to heel.

They followed the river downstream until it forked. They kept to the near side, as the river cut through the valley, passing close alongside the foothills of the mountains. Finally the path broke away from the river and headed upward, deeper into the forest. As the path climbed in elevation, Brandon began to tremble, shivering in his wet clothes.

"I'm sorry," he said, sniffling.

"That doesn't matter now," Tom said. "Just take me to him."

X.

Finally they came upon a clearing in the dense darkness of the forest. In the center of the clearing, illuminated by the cold light of the moon, Ajay lay stretched out like a starfish. The ropes, tied to his wrists and ankles, pulled his legs and arms in opposing directions toward four little trees—trees grown in awful symmetry, as if they were designed for this purpose. The ropes had been tied so taut, his limbs so fully extended, that his back barely touched the ground. Hearing them approach, Ajay screamed a muffled scream. His mouth was gagged with a white sock.

Tom dropped the belt and rushed to his son. He drew his knife and sawed at the ropes until he set him free. Tom hugged Ajay. He told him it was ok, that everything was ok, that it was all over. Ajay rubbed his raw wrists and ankles, where the rope had torn into his flesh. His breath was visible in the cold.

"Thank you," Ajay said, stammering.

Before he could stop himself, Tom began to cry. He cried as he had not cried in years. He cried, not caring, hot tears pouring from his eyes. He had rescued his son.

"I'm sorry," Brandon said quietly.

Tom turned around. The boy had not run. He was still there,

kneeling, his eyes blank as an animal. A trickle of blood, black in the moonlight, dripped from his nose.

Tom wiped away the tears with his sleeve. He thought of the police, their flashlights blazing, searching the cabins and the woods beyond, searching the river. He pictured them talking to Dave. By now, they would be searching for two missing boys. He thought of having to answer their stupid questions—of having to explain things he could not explain. He thought of the cameras watching him and how they would tell the story of what he had been forced to do—judging what they would never understand. They would call him a monster, even though he had acted only out of the most ancient, most fierce form of love. And then he thought of Ajay, tortured on this cruel rack, and of Ajay in the years to come, forever weak, afraid, and broken.

"No," Tom said, rising to his feet. "You're not sorry yet."

He walked toward the boy, towering above him. He grabbed the boy's hand and splayed out his little fingers.

———

GABRIEL MOSELEY is a writer and freelancer from Seattle. He received his MFA in fiction from UNC Wilmington and he has attended the Sewanee Writers' Conference and the Disquiet International Literary Program, among others. He was a finalist for the 2015 Sozopol Fiction Seminars Fellowship and a semi-finalist for the 2016 Disquiet International Literary Prize. His work has appeared in Stratus: Journal of Arts and Writing.

This is an Exercise in Detachment

Amy Purcell

We run ugly, me and Valentine. Pit-stained t-shirts, thrift shop track shorts, stretched out tube socks. Three miles down and Valentine pulls ahead of me, turns and runs backward, mocking my inability to keep up. It's been this way always, Valentine out front. I shout for him to slow down. He laughs, runs faster.

Along the path that follows what's left of the old Mill Creek, we pass all the perfect people wearing their technical tees and matching shorts; their bodies sweatless, their strides graceful. I despise them. They step wide off the path to avoid Valentine as he approaches, seize up on the leashes of their purebred Labradors and whatever-doodles, sensing that my twin brother is not one of them; not anymore.

Four miles and a freaked-out terrier later, he stops at the bend in the Mill Creek where the Great Blue Heron feeds each evening. We sit behind the chain-link fence and watch the bird at the far edge of the water. The sky is striped in sherbet pinks and oranges, and, in the twilight, the heron's wet wings twinkle like mercury. Valentine tells me the bird is a sign; exactly of what is still unclear but he assures me it will come to him soon, and when it does, it will be epic.

"Apocalyptic?" I ask.

"Maybe," he says.

I lean against him, our shoulders touching like they must have in the womb. As kids, we played this game where we'd walk around the house back to back, head to head, butt to butt, pretending we were Siamese Twins. He'd steal a butter knife from the kitchen and perform surgery.

"This is an exercise in detachment," he'd say in a deep professorial voice, imitating our dad. As Valentine sawed away at my arm or leg, I would scream theatrically as if the tiny ridges of the dull knife were scalpel sharp.

When he stretches out beside me on the grass, I take a closer look. His eyes, dark brown like mine, are glazed with exhaustion. His frizzy braid is nearly dreadlocked, as is his overgrown beard. I can't recall the last time he's showered—all we've been doing for days is running. His skin that once defied acne is lousy with furious scabs, and somewhere, beneath the Lithium fat and do-not-fuck-with-me scowl is my amazing, gifted brother with enough potential for the both of us—Saint Valentine.

The heron dips her yellow beak in the water and scuttles around. When she lifts her head, there's a tiny minnow wriggling between her pointed beak. She lowers the fish back into the water, then, suddenly jerks her head upward and swallows the fish whole.

We wait a good long while for her to repeat the show; she never does. Mosquitos party on our sweaty necks as a quarter moon replaces the sun.

"Ready?" he asks, looking at me as if he half recalls who I am, and I want to ask exactly when he stopped taking his meds but he is calming down now. I love this new game of ours.

"Ready," I say.

"Saint Gregory the Great," Valentine says.

"Easy. Patron of musicians and teachers. Not a martyr."

"And Saint Margaret?" he asks.

"Of Scotland or of Virgin?"

"Definitely virgin."

"Patron of pregnancy and childbirth. Swallowed by a dragon,

then beheaded."

"Very stubborn," I add as the heron flies away.

"Saint Gall then," he says.

I tell him what he already knows, that in the ninth century, Gall built a fire deep in the woods of Switzerland, and as he warmed his hands at the flames, a bear charged at him. Yet, the bear, so awed by Gall's presence, retreated into the woods to gather more firewood and join him beside the fire. The rest of his days, Gall was stalked by the bear.

"Me too," Valentine whispers. "Me too."

We were born on Valentine's Day almost nineteen years ago, Valentine first, then me—Corazón. Cory. Every birthday, Mom makes us matching cakes and gives us matching shirts, ignoring that we are not identical twins, me being a girl. On our sixteenth birthday, I got a record player and Valentine got his first stay in the psych ward after I found him preaching from the Book of Revelations on the corner of Hamilton Avenue. When we turned seventeen, we ate slices of red velvet and clacked away on our matching typewriters while Dad walked out for the proverbial ice cream and never returned. That was the same year that Dad achieved tenure at the university in—wait for it—Psychiatry.

Mom called it Achieving Torture. We couldn't disagree.

After Mom was certain Dad wasn't coming back she painted the house pink—more Pepto-Bismol than adobe—then built a shrine in the front yard. Each morning, she opens the little glass door and lights the pillar candles inside. One for Saint Jude, patron of lost causes and souls. Then Saint Anthony, patron of lost things, and Saint Dymphna, patroness of the mentally ill, and, of course, Saint Valentine, patron of love and, lesser known, of bee keepers and people with epilepsy and those plagued with any type of plague. She believes that devotions to the saints and Tibetan prayer flags and Chimayo dirt from New Mexico and holy water from Lourdes will cure Valentine. She claims mood stabilizers and psychiatrists like Dad are against all of her religions. The shrine also holds a tattered copy of Cervantes' *Don Quixote*, the untranslated version. Also plastic yellow roses in a crystal vase. Also a framed photo of Valentine from our junior year. He's on the stage in the auditorium accepting yet another award from the principal. No part of me is in the shrine. According to Mom, I don't need prayers or worship.

How I got to be an expert on the saints is through Valentine. During his second stay in the ward, one of the volunteer nuns gave him *The Lives of the Saints for Every Day of the Year* by Father Alban Butler. Apparently, she thought this would be light reading for her patients. We spent most evenings lying on his bed memorizing their miracles, their arch-enemies, how they were tortured and martyred. Achieving Torture—there are so many methods.

This last time, after Valentine binged on eBay and infomercials with Mom's credit card and the living room looked like a QVC lost and found, Dad mailed us extra cash to put Valentine in art therapy. Painting, he lectured, would be more productive than memorizing ways to die. Now Valentine paints ex-votos on things I scavenge from the thrift shop where I work part-time. Planks of wood, license plates, cardboard, toilet seats, kitchen chairs. Each ex-voto features Valentine in peril. Stabbed, shot with arrows, impaled on a stake, crushed by train, drowned in a river, struck by lightning, attacked by toothy wolves, abducted by aliens. Always, in the top left corner, he paints the saint that saves him from certain death. The newest one: Valentine shackled to a tree, a swarm of bees spouting from the top of his head. He told me his mind feels like a shaken beehive and the bees are stinging him, only the stings are his thoughts, rapid and unrelenting, and he can't get the bees organized, like they are queenless or something, and he wishes he could cut a hole in the top of his head to release them.

When I ask how I can help, he shrugs and begins to paint me, hovering over the swarm like a menacing angel.

At breakfast, Mom sets a plate of sunnyside-up eggs in front of me and another plate at Valentine's empty chair. Underneath the eggs a slice of curled bacon smiles at me.

"I'm not twelve anymore," I say, pulling the bacon mouth into a frown.

From my backpack, I pull out the *Diagnostic and Statistical Manual of Mental Disorders* for my Psych 201 class. Dad called it his Daily Source of Miracles, meaning the more disorders available, the more grant money for him. I open the giant book, the pages loosened from the spine. In the past month, I've diagnosed myself with Malingering, Caffeine Withdrawal, Generalized Anxiety Disorder, and Restless Legs Syndrome. I read aloud to Mom: "A manic episode is a period of at least one week when a person is very high-spirited or irritable in an extreme way, has more energy than usual, runs for miles and miles, paints all the time, has less need for sleep, and exhibits increased risky behavior like running and painting."

"You shouldn't read that trash," she mumbles.

"It's all right here," I say, pointing to the page where I've logged our running distances in the margins. The pile of unfinished ex-votos in the garage speak for themselves.

She stands over my shoulder and puts her hand on the page near mine. She's wearing the red kimono Dad gave to her as a Christmas gift the year he left, along with instructions to find her inner geisha girl. The sleeves are frayed, and ribbons of silk slide around her wrists, then fall onto the page. She smells of dish soap and bacon grease and easy Sunday mornings, and I want to ask her what she will do if it happens to me, if I will get a shrine too, but I'm not sure I want to hear her answer; she has always loved my brother more.

Mom waves her hand dismissively and pulls the bacon from Valentine's plate, returns it to the pan on the stove where she'll keep it warm for him forever.

"He won't eat today," I say.

"If only you'd have more faith," she sighs.

I drag my knife through the middle of the slushy yolk. Valentine and I were two separate eggs once, dizygotic twins, but I know from all the tests we've taken that we share fifty percent of our DNA so there's half a chance that any day now I could end up like him. Dad says I have nothing to worry about because we are not identical but I can't be so sure. Sometimes I lie in bed and try to conjure up the mad parade of voices, the angry bees, but they never come.

Valentine walks into the kitchen. His face is flushed and damp with sweat. He grabs a bacon strip from the pan, fresh red paint still dripping from his fingers.

"Things going well in the studio?" Mom asks.

That's what she calls the garage where he paints. Mom also calls his bipolar *creative genius*, says medications ruin his *god-given talents*.

Valentine high-fives her and she looks at her palm, now speckled red, and smiles blissfully as if she's bearing the stigmata.

"I'm on top of the world," he shouts, then glares at me.

Bright rays pour through the kitchen window and I know our run will be very long, very hard today. Valentine twists the knob on the stove until the blue flame blooms under the pan then collapses, over and over.

"I'm painting a mural on the garage."

"That's wonderful, honey," Mom says, her voice milky and warm.

"I think I saw the Virgin Mary in the bathroom tile," I say.

Mom says nothing, just gently nudges Valentine away from the stove and hands him a forkful of bacon. I dig my nails into my legs, imagine her kimono catching fire. Not even Saint Florian, patron of firefighters, would save her.

"Anyway," Valentine shouts, irritated I interrupted him. "I'm thinking like Diego Rivera out there. Big statement. None of that calla lily shit."

Mom looks at him, beaming. "Genius," she says.

He wraps his hands around my neck and begins to squeeze. "Diego had a twin brother who died."

Mom snaps the dishtowel against his arm. "No one is dying, *mi hijito.*"

He lets go of me, talking on while I slip the DSM in my backpack, pull on my running shoes. He lists Rivera's paintings, the names of his wives, something about Lenin and revolutions and his sentences become fragments as he talks faster and faster, the front door slamming against the wall so hard when he opens it that my eggs quiver.

"Just you wait," he yells. "They'll flock here for my work. Like Rivera at La Casa Azul."

I push my eggs away. They're too sad with their oozing eyes, without their bacon mouth.

"Our house is pink," I argue, but Valentine is already gone and Mom only has ears for him.

Outside, a crash. I run to the front door and watch Valentine

haul paintings from the garage, scatter them across the lawn.
"You should help your brother," Mom says.

Already the neighbors are at their windows, peeking around
the curtains as Valentine stomps about the yard, rearranges his
paintings. I force myself to look at each painting, really look.
They are disturbingly good, painfully so, and, in none of them
am I the savior. A bitter taste pushes into my mouth, and I hate
my brother a little.

"Cory, it has to be you," Mom whispers. "There's no one else."
I should want to save him again. Stop this like I've done
before but what I want instead is to be him, feel everything he
feels, think everything he thinks, have Mom turn toward me.
I'm here, I want to scream but instead I stand there, unable to
move, unable to say anything as Mom pushes me aside, waving
a crumpled twenty-dollar bill at Valentine.

At school, I sit through Psych 201 half-listening and half-guilty
that I'm not at home helping Valentine with his front yard art
fair. The class feels like it's full of students who know what they
want to do with their lives. They sit in packs, fist-bumping and
calling each other Bro and Hey Girl and Dude. Valentine was
supposed to be in class with me so I'm always turning to my left
to whisper something to him about the dreadful professor with
his elbow-patched corduroy jacket and Einstein hair, but every
time I look over the chair is empty and I feel even more lost.

In Spanish 404 where it's *no habla Ingles* for fifty-five minutes, the other students itch to get out early because it's Thirsty
Thursday and they can't wait to take their fake IDs and fake
tans and fake laughter to Uncle Woody's so they can throw up
on themselves tomorrow morning. A Dude—or maybe it's a
Bro—sits next to me and spreads his leg so his knee touches
mine. He stinks of stale sex and beer.

"Want to come to Uncle Woody's tonight?" he asks, his face
greasy with hangover. He asks in English which is against class
rules.

"*Estoy ocupado*," I say.

He cocks his head, thinks, then points toward the door.

"The bathroom is down the hall," he says.

I imagine bringing him home to Mom and Valentine but then

I think there must be more satisfying ways to Achieve Torture. Now that we're on a roll, I say, "*Me estoy volviendo loca.*" He turns toward me, his vinegar breath hanging between us. "That's so hot," he says. "I dig when girls aren't afraid to talk about their pussies."

After class, I go to the registrar's office and flip through the course catalog, then hand my student ID to the stress-pinched woman behind the desk.

"Let's drop Spanish and Psych and add Painting and Studio 1," I say brightly.

She types something into the computer, then shakes her head. "Those are only for Fine Arts majors."

"You must have my name wrong," I say. "It's Valentine. Valentine Corazón Flores."

At the thrift shop, it's my turn to work the drive-up bins. I pick up a pair of barely worn tennis shoes. They are my size, bright white with a gray Nike swoosh. Valentine's interest in running has faded now that he's moved on to painting so I have been running for both of us.

Instead of pitching the shoes in the bin filled with scuffed-up wingtips and worn-out sandals, I slip them in my backpack. Women in pearly white SUVs unload garbage bags filled with clothes that still have the price tags attached. I give them receipts for tax purposes, inform them that Saint Benedict Joseph Labre, patron of bachelors, rejects, hobos, and homeless men thanks them for their generous donations.

Dad rolls up in his Lexus like he does once a month and opens the trunk, hands me a box of baby clothes and toys—unwanted things the step-sister I've never met has outgrown.

I yank the box from him, inspect a stuffed elephant. Its yellowed tusks hang by threads and its fur is matted with dried spittle.

"Is something wrong?" he asks.

"With this?" I ask, shaking the elephant at him. "It's beyond gently used. Positively over-loved. I shouldn't accept it."

"With you," he says. He folds his arms, keeps his gaze on me the way he used to when Valentine and I served as his psychological experiments. "Is something wrong with you?"

I shrug, toss the elephant in the bin.

"Is it a boyfriend? School? Any problems there?"

"Not really."

"Doctor Thatcher said you dropped his class."

I dump all the pink baby things into the bin, watch them mix with the blue jumpers and onesies. The bin reeks of sour formula and baby powder and purity, and again, a bitter taste collects in my mouth.

"And your brother?"

I swallow hard, push the bitter taste back down. When I peeked in the garage last night, half-finished paintings leaned against the walls, on top of the workbench, on the floor—every piece of junk I'd salvaged from the shop shined with wet paint.

"Your son is grand. Brilliant! He thinks he's Diego Rivera right now."

"Should I be worried? Your mother doesn't take this seriously but if he's delusional—"

"He's already sold some paintings," I say, omitting it was Mom who bought them.

Dad runs his hands down his face. He doesn't leave so we just stand there staring into the filthy bin until another car pulls up and honks its horn.

"Listen," he says, "remember how you used to dress up like him to try to fool your teachers. Remember when your mother took you to the doctor because you were convinced you were growing a penis. No one ever wanted you to be like him, Cory. You have other things to offer."

"Like what?"

Dad frowns, pushes his shiny loafer into the pothole in the pavement.

"Things," he says, swooping his arms around the parking lot. "If you could just find a way to apply those things, Cory."

"I'm not paint," I say. "You apply paint. You apply glue. You apply butter to toast."

"I can't help you if you won't accept help."

"I'm not the one who needs help, remember? You're supposed to be helping him, not me."

Dad opens the car door.

"Cory," he says and it sounds like *sorry*. "You don't love

the broken and damaged child less because they're broken and damaged."

I watch the turn signal blink as he drives away.

"Wrong," I say. "You should love her more."

In Studio, my canvas remains blank. While the other students paint, I keep myself busy looking through art books, mixing paints. My easel is at the back of the room and, in front of me, it's all pointed elbows and hunched shoulders and very serious *artistas en el futuro*. I pull a small frame from my backpack and set it next to the giant white block of nothing on my easel. Inside the frame is one of Valentine's ex-votos. Before class, I'd gone to the garage, told Valentine that I needed a hammer and when he didn't turn away from his work, I grabbed the frame nearest the door and left.

Now I look at the image for the first time. There's the Mill Creek filled with green-gray water and the Great Blue Heron dressed in fine robes like the Pope. The sky is angry red instead of blue and, trapped in the heron's beak is Valentine without a head. Standing next to the bird is me with my brother's head raised above me like a hat I'm about to wear. Instead of blood, tears drip from Valentine's head onto my face and shoulders, a black puddle surrounding my feet. Up in the left corner, I immediately recognize Saint Cecelia, organ pipes in hand, her severed head resting on her shoulder. Patron of musicians, she of the stubborn head. Her executioner tried to behead her three times, but still they could not decapitate her so she lived for three more days as people soaked up her blood with cloths and squirreled it away hoping for miracles. I can't decide whether I'm supposed to be happy or sad that Valentine has given me his head. The professor passes behind me and looks at Valentine's painting with me.

"You should steal that," she says. "Good artists imitate and great artists steal."

I dip my brush in red paint and press the bristles onto the canvas but my hand is shaking and I know whichever way I move, it will be wrong; it is all wrong.

On Sunday, I dawdle around the house, avoiding Mom and my

homework. I fold laundry, rearrange my running shirts, try my new Nikes on again. They are real running shoes for real runners, and I squish-squish, spring-spring across the linoleum in the kitchen. When I think Valentine has painted long enough, I knock on the garage door. No answer. I knock again, then walk toward him, hitch my Nike-clad foot onto his knee.

"Time to run," I say all sing-song.

"Go away," he murmurs.

I do a couple of calf stretches and squats. My legs are muscular now, almost boyish, and, for once, I am sure I can outrun my brother.

"I'm working," he says.

"Come on," I whine. "Just this once."

Valentine rolls his eyes, reluctantly grabs his old Converse. He gets up from the chair slowly. He looks old and weary and already beaten.

We run through Spring Grove Cemetery. I feel great. I feel strong and now it's Valentine trying to keep up. I run like a stiff-legged zombie, lurching toward other visitors yelling, "brains, brains." I hear Valentine behind me, laughing. It is the best sound of all. We are twins again, *Valentine y Corazón contra el mundo*!

With Valentine far behind, I reach the Mill Creek alone, and pump my fists in the air as I cross my imaginary finish line. In the distance, I see the heron slowly gliding above the creek, her wings arched and taut, her long legs like two sharp arrows as she lands at the edge of the water. The ducks paddle away from her as if her spot is sacred. I want her to look up and see me behind the chain-link fence, recognize that, today, I am winning. I spread my arms like wings and think of Saint Francis, how the doves perched on his hands and shoulders. I wish for the heron to fly to me, but she doesn't move.

I feel Valentine approach behind me, hear him panting. I begin to turn around to claim my victory but he shoves me backward, pins me against the fence. There are bags under his eyes and a desperate wildness I've seen in his face just a few other times. I try to break free but he is enormous, stronger now that something cruel, this unwelcome stranger, is overtaking him. He will not remember this later; he never does. I wait for the punch, for the kick in my gut, the crack of bone that has come when we've reached this point before. I wait, chain-metal pressing a honeycomb pattern into my back. I wait, gasping for air as he pins my chest, my arms. I wait for my brother to return to himself. I wait to become someone—anyone—else.

"Saint Juliana," I squeak. "Patron of chronic suffering. Saint Aloyisius, patron of caregivers."

He presses harder. "Fuck your stupid games, Cory. Just fuck you."

And then his face softens and he groans. The sound is ancient and bottomless.

"It's over. *Terminado*," he says.

A familiar spasm of panic creeps through me, a dizzy feeling, like I shouldn't press him any farther because I don't want to hear what comes next.

"Don't talk like that," I manage to say.

"You're the death of me," he says, his voice as thin as the air left in my lungs.

He frees my arms and I grab his hands. They feel so heavy and under the heaviness, I feel the crushing gloom, the long descent into the deep well and, for the first time, it occurs to me that he is trying to protect me from falling down with him. My brother has not been running away from me but running toward something I will never feel or achieve; this is the torture for both of us.

When I finally reach home, the door to the garage is half-open. Light leaks onto the driveway. All the houses on the street are dark except ours and the air holds the suggestion of rain. I peek around the door and see Valentine lying on the old couch, his arms measled with bright patches of paint. His hair, unbraided, falls about his shoulders in squally curls. I stand next to him long enough for him to notice my presence in the room, that I am not an illusion. He puts his hands over his face, blue fingerprints dotting his cheeks.

I can't look at my broken brother on the couch any longer. On the easel is a piece of wood with two beatific faces gazing back at me, their eyes disproportionately huge. A tiny pink house perched on a hill at their feet. The figures each have Valentine's face yet I know they are the martyred twins, Saints Benedict and Scholastica—the first saint story we memorized. Benedict looks most like Valentine, the hair, the beard, the dark eyes. Scholastica, who should have my face, appears nearly the same as Benedict, yet her body is a grotesque Dali jumble of splintered double helixes.

I search for my face, my likeness, among the dismembered bodies and skeletal remains that are stacked against the pink house and find it nowhere until I see the Great Blue Heron, positioned where Valentine usually paints his saint and savior. There I am, hanging from the heron's talons, limp and dead, a ghostly veil.

Something unspools inside me, like wings unfurling to catch the wind.

Outside, it begins to rain. Water sloshes out of the clogged gutters and waterfalls onto Mom's tomato plants. The candles flicker in the shrine as if they are laughing at the storm.

"It's perfect," I say to Valentine. "Really."

I sit beside my brother on the old couch, the space between us like another living thing.

AMY PURCELL has been published in Third Coast, Beloit Fiction Journal, Timber Creek Review, The Writer Magazine, and other literary journals. She holds an MFA in Creative Writing from Kent State University and a B.S. in Magazine Journalism from Ohio University. She lives in Cincinnati, Ohio with her husband, David, and their two Australian Shepherds, Macy and Seamus. Amy has worked in corporate communications for more than twenty-five years and is currently the Corporate Storyteller for Fifth Third Bancorp. When she's not working on her novel, you can find her running or reading. Amy has never met a craft beer or potato chip she didn't love. As evidenced by her closets, she should have been a shoe designer.

Hope Gold

Leslie Jones

Cold drizzle spattered the strip mall parking lot. Steve hurried under the awning in sour anticipation. He glimpsed his own frowning mustache in the window glass of the satellite phone store. The door bells jingled, but the mouse-haired gal behind the counter barely nodded in his direction, too busy staring at the phone in her hand. She was holding a regular cell phone, not one of the bedeviled pieces of shit they'd sold him last year. The store had gray carpet and fluorescent overheads. He'd probably have wound up a hopeless case like Lou if he had to spend all day in a place like this. Could definitely see that.

"Can I help you?" she finally asked.

"I don't know. You tell me." He tossed his satellite phone on the counter, rattling the glass. "This thing is showing the wrong date. I was out in Hope last weekend, could barely get it to work. See here." He pointed to the date on the analog screen with his crooked pinky, the one he'd smashed on a trailer hitch long ago on that godforsaken dairy farm. "This thing says it's April 18, 2009. That's way before I even bought this phone."

She took it off the counter and pressed buttons until a blinking circle of dots appeared on the screen. "It should work now," she said. A minute later, the normal screen returned. "There." She pointed to the corrected display. "The software update from last November caused about one in five phones to have issues, but I've installed the latest version. You're good to go."

Her singsong satisfaction steamed him. His satellite phone was important survival gear. "So you knew there was a problem and you didn't tell anyone? I was out in Hope, I had an emergency and could barely get this thing to work."

"They issued an update as soon as they found out about it," she said.

He imagined the spinning black dots on the analog screen blinking in her pea brain. "I pay you people two hundred bucks every six months just *in case* I need to use this thing. You had an issue affecting a bunch of customers and didn't say so?"

"Hardly anyone had a problem."

"What about the ones who did? Did you ever think about sending a letter?" He pressed his fingers to the sides of his head and pushed off in a firework motion, gesturing to the stupidity of this entire operation.

"Well, we did email everyone at the time, but that was two updates ago, sir. You should always install every new update."

The door bells clanged violently behind him. One of the damnedest things about this life was that you could be a self-made man—grow up on a poor dairy farm getting walloped by your old man, beat tracks north as fast as you could, work construction in thirty-below, the snow going sideways, balls freezing off. You could help build the state's vital artery, the greatest feat of modern engineering on the planet—eight hundred miles of steel pipeline with capacity to cradle two million rushing barrels of Prudhoe Bay crude oil. You could make a pile, lose it, become a plumber, start a business, provide good steady jobs for six people, pay your taxes and still, *still* have to endure people who did not value hard work. They were everywhere in Anchorage these days, easily spotted behind the city's cash registers—the undermotivated and underemployed. Young people, mostly. The only thing their generation had over his was easy understanding of every new electronic doohickey. They lorded it over old guys like him with thoughtless exasperation, and an eyeball roll, "Oh it's easy, just press this." He couldn't stand it. He plopped into his work van and checked his cell. There was a text from his older sister Janine.

Heard anything from him? she wrote.

Steve tapped *n-o*. Janine lived about an hour's drive from Lou, but Steve was closer to him in age, only fifteen months older than their youngest sibling. He'd always taken an interest in Lou, tried to set him on the right path. The responsibility had fallen on his shoulders after Dad's death. Over the decades, in many attempts, he'd tried to interest Lou in turning a profit. He'd even invited Lou up to take a crack at his new hobby out at Hope.

He popped the middle console and reached between CD cases for the Altoids tin where he kept his happy thought. He stuck his thumb under the metal ridge and the lid clicked back, revealing the dusting of hearty yellow flakes clinging to the edges. By today's price ($1,320 an ounce), he was looking at about three hundred dollars. He kept most of his haul at home in a plastic container tucked in a drawer behind a pile of wool socks. He hoped to find enough to get little bars made at the end of the season, stamped with ONE OUNCE FINE HOPE GOLD, and a logo of his girlfriend Trudy's creation. She was working on a sketch of a splashing whale tail. He liked that, flukes flapping on the wealth they'd pulled out of Hope's dirt. It wasn't like the old days. He knew old timers who'd kept years' worth of nuggets in coffee tins until the price shot up. Then they bought themselves nice boats. He'd once seen a miner tip a stripper with a pennyweight nugget. That was back when more guys open carried and people snorted coke right off the tables at Chilkoot Charlie's. Alaska wasn't like that anymore. Gold mining was a rugged pastime, but no longer a path to fortune for a small-claim prospector like himself. Nevertheless, he and Trudy were making out pretty good this season. He had already recouped the cost of renting the dredge, and wanted to work out a percentage for her. He'd paid all the upfront costs, but Trudy was a big help, had put in a lot of weekends. She laughed off all his suggestions though, said she was just there to enjoy his company and summer weather, that she liked him as a boyfriend, not a business partner. Her brush-offs bothered him. He hated debts of any kind. He put the tin back and phoned her. He told her about the text from Janine.

"Are you going to call him?" Trudy asked.

"Why? He said not to."

"I know, but maybe he didn't mean it." That was Trudy, always thinking of others. She didn't really understand about dealing with Lou, though Steve had explained a good deal. She was always trying to get Steve to see Lou as a product of history and circumstance. There wasn't anything to be done about the past, but Steve believed every man was responsible for changing his own life. He told Trudy he'd pick her up for happy hour at five.

If anyone deserved sympathy it was *Trudy*, not Lou. She ran her own business distributing quilt fabrics to craft stores statewide. Every year got harder, with more people buying their supplies online or from box stores carrying cheap bolts from China. Trudy was not much younger than him. She had a house she wanted to pay off and a kid still in high school, so she didn't buy health insurance. He understood the gamble, but then she slipped on the ice last winter, busted her knee, and had to pay out of pocket. No one told her that she could have asked the hospital to only charge what they'd get from Medicare for the surgery. It set her back on the house. Trudy was someone who took care of herself and didn't complain or blame anyone when she was dealt a shit hand. He was mad at Lou on her account: she was still limping, but being a good sport, helping out, going over the sluice box, looking for shiny flecks, fixing ham sandwiches for lunch. They were having a great time, and then Lou ruined it from two thousand miles away.

In more than one past relationship, the final feedback was that Steve wasn't an open person. He was trying to do different by Trudy. He made a point of doing the sensitive things: cooking her his special beef-stuffed bell peppers; remembering to ask about her day and concentrating on what she said; and, though he disliked talking about himself, he was trying to do more of it, to *build intimacy*, because Trudy was a remarkable and beautiful woman. He wanted her to stick around. He didn't care for childhood reminiscing, but it seemed a natural place to start. He'd already told her how he'd tried to teach Lou the value of a dollar since back when they were two Oregon farm kids. He'd recalled for her how he and Lou used to play pirates in the forest beyond the pasture. Their ship was a felled Douglas Fir. Steve was captain, being older. Scallop shells and sand dollars scavenged on the old man's grudging, infrequent family beach trips were their treasure. There was always a reason not to go to the beach, something else to do on the farm. They kept the shells in a mossy depression covered with branches. Dad was always saying nothing ever came easy, to guard tightly whatever they had.

Steve remembered waking up the morning after the Columbus Day storm. Dad was yelling *goddamn it all to hell* in the kitchen. Steve pulled back their bedroom window curtain. Part of the fence was blown over, lumber scattered in the driveway. He'd wondered even then if it was the damage riling Dad. Cows were fine. No one hated the cows more than Dad. Somehow the kids convinced him to drive them out to the coast. Steve was surprised that he agreed. Dad probably wanted to rubberneck; he could get deliciously preoccupied with other peoples' misfortune. Mom wanted to stay home and clean up, but relented when Dad hustled everyone into the truck. They had to skirt tree boughs and debris on the road.

The three kids spilled out of the backseat and down to the shore. Mom followed slowly with a bag for picking up garbage. Dad leaned on the hood and waited. There were buoys and cartons, huge seaweed-wrapped chunks of driftwood, lots of trash. Steve found a crab pot, three shell casings, and a soggy magazine with a picture of a big blonde in frilly underwear. He was worrying over how to get her home, afraid if he folded the page in his pocket he'd ruin it, when Lou came running.

"Look everybody!" Lou cried. Elbows locked beside his ears, hands high in the air, he held up an enormous glass float, perfectly round, bigger than his head. He pushed it up like he was giving it to the sky. The sun broke through the clouds, beaming on the pale green orb. Mom and Janine cheered. In Steve's memory, even Dad nodded from the top of the sand. Lou knew it. The wind blew back his blond hair, and he smiled with his whole face, missing his front teeth at the time—he'd found the best thing on the beach.

They stopped at the only open store on the way home so Dad could buy smokes. Mom waited in the car while Steve,

Janine, and Lou followed Dad in and crowded the candy rack. Steve had some money he'd earned caring for their neighbor's chickens. Janine had money too, since she was old enough to babysit. Lou didn't. Already, even back then, Steve had told Trudy, you could see the pattern developing. Lou asked Steve to lend him a quarter, and he almost did before he remembered the glass float in the trunk.

"If I sell it to you, can I buy it back later?" Lou wanted to know. He had a powerful sweet tooth, a precursor to more ruinous cravings.

"Sure, but the cost might change."

"Well, probably not much, right?"

Steve shrugged.

"Careful, Lou," Janine warned. "Stevie'll take you to the cleaners." She paid for her M&Ms and walked out to the car. Of course she'd warn their youngest brother off, but not lend him anything herself.

Dad watched as Steve paid for Astro Pops and taffy. Lou took his share and skipped out to the car. Dad grabbed Steve's shoulder. "Don't give it back to him," he said.

"What?"

"That brother of yours can't think more than five seconds ahead. He's got to learn."

Steve kept the float under his bed in the room they shared, although Lou had no doubt expected he'd add it to their treasure pile in the woods. Lou offered twice, then three times, as much as Steve had paid for candy. Dad shook his head with a smirk, winking at Steve over the back of Lou's head, when Lou pleaded with Steve at dinner. Steve had no choice but to hold fast; he knew that Dad's scorn would reroute toward him if he gave in and returned the float to Lou.

"Just tell me what the amount is, and I'll start saving up," Lou said in bed that night.

Lou's anxious questions started to annoy Steve, especially since floats weren't even worth that much. They washed up all the time. Lou had no sense, selling too low, then asking Steve to name his price. Steve thought of a way to extend the lesson. He hadn't told Trudy this part, because it embarrassed him a little, even after all these years.

"Why don't you start by shoveling the pen for me tomorrow," Steve said.

"Then I can have it back?"

"I didn't say that."

Lou sighed and rolled toward the wall, but the next morning Steve watched him heft the shovel, taller than he was, and ladle cow pies into a bucket. After that it was easy to get Lou to do chores, and in the woods, Steve ordered him about in the fort building. He got Lou to give up his half of the seashells. Lou seemed to forget the score entirely, as if the mission all along was just to make Steve happy. Steve couldn't remember how it ended. Mom must've noticed and told him to quit taking advantage of his brother. The float stayed under Steve's bed until he left home. He didn't remember any bitterness from Lou. Mostly he remembered the two of them poking slugs with sticks and pulling up fistfuls of ferns to make clearings for their forts. All that tromping in the woods was in the back of Steve's mind when he took up gold mining. He'd asked Lou to come up and help. They weren't kids anymore; Steve would've cut him in on any profits, above operating costs.

Steve drove out of the parking lot, headed to a house call on the hillside. He punched the radio knob to silence the a.m. talk show and let his mind hover on Lou. Like a wheel spinning in air, his thoughts cycled through the years, each spoke a point of divergence: Steve's life moved ahead while Lou's went nowhere. Steve had done all he could. Probably too much. Maybe if there'd been more tough love, Lou would've turned out better. Trudy would disagree with him there. She'd said that in her experience, tough love was just potting soil for resentment.

Dad drank even harder during Steve's last year at home. He banged around the house, cuffed whoever was within arm's reach. Janine was already gone, moved a whole state away to wait tables in Boise. One evening Dad plowed Steve's head against a doorframe. His offense had been a disrespectful "yeah" and an eye roll when Dad slurrily asked if Steve had added fresh sawdust to the cow pens. Steve's head ached for hours after. Nighttime was worst. The old man was most volatile after dark. Steve got a job at the movie theater that kept him away most evenings. He couldn't wait to get out of the house. Lou, being the youngest, might have got more than his share of Dad's knocks. It hadn't been good to leave Lou at home, but Lou was old enough then, he could've got a job too. Then Mom would've had to endure Dad alone. Steve was no hero. Everyone commends the brave older sibling who sacrifices himself to the father-tyrant. Those are the stories that get told. What of the one who looked out for his own skin? Less inspiring, but probably more common than the courageous type, Steve reckoned. An article in *Time* said they were paying guys a thousand dollars a week to build an oil pipeline in Alaska. In an interlude of sobriety, Dad told Steve it looked like a good idea: everyone knew there was money up there, and even if his son had to live in an igloo, it'd beat a lifetime of stinking goddamn milk cows. Steve left the day after graduation, told Lou to come along next year.

Steve was skunked his first two weeks in Fairbanks. The whole country wanted a pipeline job. On the advice of a guy staying at the same flophouse, he paid off the union man with his savings. Flew to camp four days later. Ten-, twelve-hour days, he and the other workers fed four-foot-wide galvanized steel pipe into vertical supports. They obliterated the rest of waking time with jug vodka and Schlitz. Steve drank even more when the wind blew a certain way and made the toilet trailers stink like the farm. Everybody partied. Working in the middle of nowhere was boring and everyone had more money than ever before. Steve steered clear of the drugs, but partook of other distractions on his R&R trips to Fairbanks, where the Second Avenue bars were filled with hookers from all over. They'd come up to strike it rich, same as the pipeline workers. At first he went with ones who resembled girls from back home, but realized he liked them older and bigger, liked getting lost in tits and flesh. Plus the older ones didn't eyeball him like he was a puzzle in need of putting together. The guys ribbed him for chubby chasing. He didn't care. He was nineteen and, with so much overtime, making more than Dad ever had, earning more even than a sitting congressman. Days became weeks and months. Winter came. The windchill factor defied the living, and then a phone call from Mom. She said Dad had died. Heart attack. She told him to find a flight home for the funeral.

Probably shouldn't have been a surprise. There were no days off in dairy farming. Every time the old man cursed a cow, threw a tool, or kicked a barn or bucket seemed posthumously justified. At home, Lou said Dad had slumped over watching *Wheel of Fortune* and that was it. But everybody knew it was the farm that did him in.

Steve thought the long trip home would dry him out, but he felt shaky during the service at the Baptist church. The whole family's attendance had been irregular there, nobody's more so than Dad's. Steve wondered anxiously if the extended family packed into the pews could smell or otherwise detect that he'd spent the last eight months becoming a degenerate. He didn't cry. He peeked at Lou who looked shell-shocked but not sad. Janine stared at nothing, like she was at a bus station, waiting to board. Steve felt guilty on behalf of all three of them. Their father wasn't perfect, but it was egregious to think ill of the dead, especially with him not even in the ground. And hadn't Dad done his best to put food on the table, suffer his work, and provide? Surely he'd tried, in his way, to do the right thing. Steve resolved to pick up where Dad had left off. He started by asking Lou, again, to come to Alaska.

"I'll even loan you money for the plane ticket," Steve told him. Everybody was back at the house.

"Sure, thanks, I'll think about it." Lou took his plate and went to sit by Mom in the living room.

Steve couldn't quite figure out their closeness. Maybe he should've pushed it further, but he knew somehow that Lou wouldn't be coming.

Steve spent two years on the pipeline, in three different camps. He'd put a decade's worth of miles on his liver, and had just enough cash in his bank account to keep making truck payments. It was the same for everyone. When crude came swishing down the pipeline, the oil companies shed a lot of union labor. Steve couldn't blame them, from what he'd seen and done. Boys in another part of the world might be sent out to spear a lion. Steve severed his childhood by drinking and fucking and forcing the earth to deliver its wealth to the nation. Without a regret or hard feeling, he slapped a bumper sticker on his truck: *Please God give us one more Prudhoe Bay, I promise not to piss this one away.*

With the oil running, plus the billion-dollar payout the federal government fed to the Alaska Native corporations, there was money flying around everywhere. You didn't need many brains to catch some of it. Steve worked construction in Anchorage, took the necessary courses, found a journeyman to work under, saved money, started his own plumbing company, and never looked back. By the time he was successful enough to offer Lou an apprenticeship, Mom was sick. Janine was married and living an hour away. Steve didn't know what Lou had been doing back home, but now Lou was determined to stay. It was noble and all, but no one had asked him to. Steve had gone back three times before Mom died, and she was a little weaker each time. Lou had taken on more around the house—the laundry, the kitchen, her prized vegetable garden. They'd sold the cows shortly after Dad passed, so Lou hitched his ambitions to a health and human services certification through the local community college, but no county job emerged. Lou blamed budget cuts, but Steve suspected his DUIs had something to do with it. Mom let him know that much before she went. Steve bawled Lou out, but what could he do?

They sold the farm two months after her death. Lou wrote a letter to both Janine and Steve after the funeral, proposing he stay on and slowly buy them out. Really, he couldn't afford it, working gas station jobs and the like, especially with the property market soaring. He sometimes had girlfriends, but they never lasted. Lou only ever found ones with bad debts or troublemaking exes. Each had some problem Lou couldn't save her from, but that never stopped him trying, even if it meant miring himself in a money jam or suffering some dip-lipped redneck idling in his truck in Lou's condo parking lot, trying to figure out if his woman was holed up there. Steve thought Lou should get a gun. Count that as one more piece of untaken advice. Lou couldn't be moved to stake his claim in the world; he wouldn't even commit to defending what little washed his way.

Steve went back every year or two. They'd sit in the cramped kitchen in Lou's little condo drinking coffee, hardly saying anything. Mom, Janine, the changes in town. Those were their usual conversation topics. They never talked about Dad. Like Steve, Lou had a full mustache, but his was lighter. They were built the same, bulky through the chest and shoulders, lean-legged. But Lou was somehow more brittle. They were like copies from the same Xerox, only the machine ran low on ink when the time came to print out Lou: he was missing lines and impossible to read. Steve planned his trips around hunting season. Over the years he perfected his travel routine so that he was in town for the big family meal. Sometimes they drove together to eat at Janine's. Her house was too loud and crowded for Lou or Steve to stand it for long, so other times she packed her husband and three kids into her van for the hour drive back home and they all ate at the nice hotel. Steve always shared a brotherly catch-up breakfast with Lou, but with the farm sold to Californian retirees, each reunion was tinged by loss, as if by giving up the acreage they'd surrendered their common ground. They were less familiar to one another away from the farm, sitting in Lou's dim living room or in a diner booth, where omelets and hash browns offset the stilted conversation. Lou didn't like to hunt. Steve spent most of these trips alone in the woods.

Steve wasn't neglectful. He called Lou every month, always asked how he was doing. The answers almost never changed, until the time, years ago now, Lou said, "Well, I took up oil painting."

Oil painting? He may as well have said belly dancing. But he told Steve he'd taken some classes, that he liked painting the beach, the street view from his living room window. He also liked painting old photos, pictures of Mom's garden, the huckleberry bushes below the old mailbox, sunlight on the front walk. It was an odd hobby, more still because Lou was preoccupied with their childhood home, a place Steve thought about so little that sometimes he wondered if he even really remembered it. Steve began asking about the painting every time he called, always wanting to know Lou's plans. Lou finally sent him a painting one Christmas: the old house, cows at pasture in the background. Steve hung it in the bathroom. People laughed when he told them his brother was a painter and where he'd hung his work. The joke belied his feelings. It was more complicated. The colors were nice. The bathroom wall allowed him more time to contemplate it than other spaces in his house. Steve noted the intricate detail of the flower boxes and Mom's shake-roof birdhouse. By comparison, the cows were blurry, the fence posts no more than quick dashes. Lou had painted it as if it were Mom's home, which was strange. Steve had always thought of it as Dad's house. Everyone else just lived there, abiding by the old man's rules. It was ludicrous, painting. He shook his head, flushed. *That brother of mine.*

Nevertheless, he pushed Lou toward the imperative that seemed to evade his brother, even in middle age: making money. If he realized the futility of painting scenes from the past, maybe he'd move on to some worthwhile endeavor. What was the end game? Steve didn't know much about art, but Lou's wasn't the kind of stuff they put in museums. The message eventually stuck. On one of his calls, Lou told him his artwork was up for sale at a coffee shop.

"How much you asking?" Steve inquired.

"Forty, sixty, somewhere in there."

"That's it?"

"Owner said that's the range folks tend to buy something."

"How long does one take you?"

"One painting?"

"Uh-huh."

"Depends. I spend a month or so on ones like I sent you, but those I'm not selling. The owner thinks people will like my beach scenes. One of those probably takes six to ten."

"Hours?" Steve's jaw dropped. He held the phone away from his mouth for a moment and swung his head around. "Forty dollars for ten hours? You know that's how much I make in fifteen minutes?"

From then on, when he called Lou he'd casually mention something he'd bought for forty dollars. Soon it was a compulsion. Every time he talked to Lou, he listed his purchases: Forty dollars on gas for the generator, new snow machining gloves, beers for his employees, fancy synthetic long johns, the masseuse who worked out the knot in his shoulder, the Super Bowl betting pool with his hunting buddies, on and on. Forty was nothing. Why pour so much time into nothing?

Steve drove the van down the highway to the Huffman exit and ascended the hillside to a bumpy gravel road. His house call that afternoon wound up being to one of those cabin-mansions Steve was partial to, a three-story A-frame with natural-wood siding. More house than he could afford. But also the kind of place poised for a big price dive, with all the oil company lay-offs. Soon there'd be way fewer people around with the means. The wife showed him to the kitchen with the dripping faucet. It took no time at all to change out the washer. He charged for the whole hour anyways. He had overhead, and that was how it worked. Two hundred bucks for something so simple was not much different than charging fourteen thousand for a routine knee surgery. But that was the way of things. Until somebody devised a better system, everyone just got reamed. The woman thanked him for his time. He asked to use the bath-room. He didn't have to go, but when he came back out he said he'd noticed her showerhead and asked if she'd considered a thermostatic system. They made them now with LED lights and rain effect, easily turning a humdrum bathroom into a spa experience, *and* more affordable than ever. She tilted her head and smiled, which he took as a good sign. He left her a product catalog and his business card, making a show of writing his cell number on it before handing it over. Then he headed back down the mountain to pick up Trudy.

He found a spot close to the front of her building. She'd said to text from the parking lot, but he walked up anyways to see if she needed help carrying anything. He hated how her leg still bothered her, seemed almost criminal after spending all that money.

"Knock-knock." He rapped on the frame to her one-room office.

Trudy looked up. Her face eased into a smile, eyes crinkling, graying blonde curls spraying off the mussy bun on her head and going everywhere. "Hello-hello." Piles of fabric lined the walls. The space smelled spicy and sweet from the jar candle on her desk. He especially liked the panel quilt hanging behind her: twelve squares each depicting a different Alaskan animal— moose, puffin, lynx, bald eagle. She appreciated the outdoors as much as he did. That was what had torpedoed his first marriage: *She didn't like hunting!* he'd told everyone, and lo and behold Trudy walked into his life equipped with her own gun closet. He'd lost count of the times he'd made the joke, until Trudy put a hand on his arm and said that surely that wasn't the full story. But who wanted the full story? Did Trudy really want to hear how he'd worn down his ex? How he'd hammered his logic over her feelings? Sometimes about big things, like not moving Outside when the economy and tax structure was so great in Alaska, but more frequently about stupid stuff. Not conveying enthusiasm when, at age forty-two, she took up the time suck of attempting a college degree. Refusing to buy the hormone-free dairy because it cost more and was a big scam anyways. Finally his wife did what he couldn't have imagined—what Mom had never even threatened to do—she left.

Trudy pushed back her chair and limped over. Her hips brushed the desk and fabric. He loved her ample softness, the way the curves of her thighs pushed against her jeans.

He set his hands on her waist and stooped for a kiss. "You ready?" he asked.

"Yep."

"Need me to grab anything?"

"Not unless you want to carry my purse"—she gave him a look—"Relax, Steve. I got it."

In the car, she let down her hair and uncapped a honey-smelling Chap Stick. "Did you call him?" she asked.

"Who?" He paused and glanced, catching her look of reproach. "I'll call him this weekend."

She sighed.

"Look," he said. "Janine calls every day. He never answers, and she's the one who picked him up after. The guy gets more attention than he deserves."

He'd been with Trudy almost two years. Disagreements could go unspoken. He knew she thought he should call; he was closer to Lou than Janine. That was exactly why Steve wouldn't. He wished she understood. Somehow she didn't, and not for his lack of trying. He'd dribbled out most of the history, was probably starting to repeat himself. He wished she'd say, *Steve, stop worrying about him. You did the best you could.* Then maybe he could cease replaying the same memories, a loop that whirled free from the friction of meaning. The reasoning that had guided Steve's life and made him a success was a smooth plane. Lou's circumstance had no traction. His little brother had failed to face reality and help himself. He'd made his own misery. When they were almost to the bar, Steve thought of a story Trudy hadn't heard yet.

"Did I ever tell you about when Janine wanted everybody to go to San Antonio for her birthday?"

"No."

"Oh yeah, we had all these emails, back and forth, trying to pick a hotel, and of course Lou won't chime in *at all*. We both know he doesn't have the money. So finally Janine says what the hell and buys his ticket. And you know what?"

"What?"

"He got tanked and missed his flight. Didn't bother to call anyone until three in the afternoon."

"Maybe he couldn't afford the hotel."

"He was supposed to room with me."

"Maybe he was embarrassed, I mean even to be around you guys."

Steve wiped the air with his hand, nosed into the parking lot. "Damned if you do, damned if you don't with that guy." He shifted into park and looked over.

Trudy rolled her head over so her chin rested on her shoulder, quiet just long enough to unsettle him. "Boy, am I ready for a margarita." She unbuckled and eased out on to the asphalt.

Steve popped the middle console and stuck the Altoids tin in his shirt pocket, thinking his regular waitress Rhonda might like a peek.

They sat down and Rhonda came by looking, as usual, like a weathered Woodstock princess, her gray hair in two long braids swinging down the front of her work shirt. She brought him his usual coffee and a brandy and Trudy her margarita. Then she asked if they'd seen the big *Alaska Dispatch News* headline— the permanent fund dividend crisis. The politicians were saying the state could no longer afford its annual oil-profit payouts to every Alaskan man, woman, and child.

"According to the Constitution," Steve started in. "The resources of the land are disposed to the people of the state, to do with as they see fit—"

"But everybody needs to contribute," Rhonda cut in. She'd served him as long as he'd been coming, had a good head on her shoulders, even if she was a lefty.

"That's fine. I do not disagree. But until I see every state worker take a hit, don't tell the family fisherman in Naknek or Cordova, the one paying Obamacare premiums on his seven kids, that they're not getting their PFD." He enjoyed getting into it with Rhonda on the old politics. He always tipped the same, even when she managed to piss him off.

Trudy twisted her wrists. Her bracelets clinked.

"You can gut the schools, Steve," Rhonda slapped a stack of cocktail napkins on the table. "But you still need to educate the kids coming up now. Oil's not coming back." She glided away from their table.

He took a loud sip of coffee. The bitterness matched the sour spot in his stomach. True, the pipeline he'd built now took eighteen days to transport oil from the North Slope to Valdez. In peak times it was four, but production had been slowing for going on two decades. Low capacity meant low speed.

Workers from the nearby office tower started trickling in, but the bar didn't fill up like it used to. BP layoffs. Now Shell was packing out of the Chukchi Sea. Everybody, every last barmaid in town, was going to feel the hurt. He looked over at Rhonda, he could see even now she wasn't busy. He waved her back over.

"Well if education's so important, wish your schools could've done a better job with the bozo in the satellite phone store I had to deal with today." Steve recounted the gal's blank stare when he told her he had an emergency in Hope.

Of course then Rhonda wanted to know about it. Steve felt the Altoids tin pressing on his chest. Trudy was rubbing the salt off the rim of her glass.

"You want to hear about my emergency?" Steve sighed. It might be a pretty funny story, depending on how he told it. "Trudy and I were out in Hope, at our site"—

"Site?" Rhonda asked. "Like a mining claim? Didn't know there was still gold out there."

"Plenty! I only go for the stuff big enough for tweezers, but they also got what they call flour gold. You can see it, makes the dirt shine. I've watched videos about how they extract it"—

"Sounds like a pain in the ass," Rhonda said. "This what he makes you do all weekend?" she asked Trudy.

"Yes," Trudy said.

"All right all right all right! Anyway, we're at the site and I still have signal enough for texts, and I get one from my brother Lou, sent to me and my sister. Here, I'll just read it to you." He took his phone out and scrolled, he then read in a melodramatic tone: "*Dear Brother and Sister; know that I love both of you, even though we don't really know each other. I've tried my hardest and I'm done trying. Be well, I won't be seeing you.*" Steve glanced up.

Rhonda and Trudy looked at one another.

"So then," Steve went on, "and I'm too far out, bad reception, can't call out, and I gotta use the satellite phone to call my sister—she lives closer. Took three calls just to make her understand it was me because the damned sat phone wasn't working right. After I got hold of her, I text Lou back, asked him why it is I won't be seeing him, and he says because he's going to be with Mom. So then I ask him what about the family reunion we got planned for Thanksgiving, cuz I'm trying to get him away from . . . that kind of thinking."

Rhonda's face was flat.

"Trudy here wanted to drive back to town, but I said no, I'm not leaving Hope. Whatever he's gonna do, I can't stop it from Anchorage."

Rhonda nodded, but looked skeptical.

"And we've been through this with Lou before. He's rotated through both of us. We've both chipped in on his mortgage more than once." Steve glanced at Trudy. "I've helped him out with his bills this year. Now he calls asking for this, that, and the other."

Recognition seeped into Rhonda's face. Everyone had a relative like that.

"So my sister Janine calls the cops—you want to hear the next text Lou sent us?" Steve made his voice even drippier: "*Dear Siblings, thanks for calling the cops. Now I am in jail and*

*will lose my job since I was supposed to be there at seven a.m.
tomorrow. Please do not contact me again.*" Steve screwed up
his mustache and shrugged.

Rhonda laughed. "They took him to jail?" she wiped her eyes.

"Where else they gonna put him?" Steve said. "But hey, he
got to keep his phone."

"Ha!" Rhonda laughed, then left to take care of another table.

Trudy changed the subject to the quilting business. She said
she was having a time meeting the demand for tropical novelty
prints. Steve stared into the dregs of his coffee. He felt a small
bubble of guilt, no bigger than a baby's burp, for making fun
of Lou. So he was younger when things went south at home.
Whatever went wrong was only a difference of degree from what
the rest of them had endured, and Lou'd passed on plenty of
chances to get the hell out. As recently as last Christmas: Steve
mailed him a card with a print out of his mileage statement,
circled the balance and wrote—*buy you a round-trip! Anytime!*
Appealing to Lou's sensitive nature, he'd even included a print
out of Robert Service's *The Spell of the Yukon*. Steve didn't
care for poetry much, but he liked this one because it talked
about adventuring north to get rich. The verses spoke to him
personally:

> *There's gold, and it's haunting and haunting;*
>   *It's luring me on as of old;*
> *Yet it isn't the gold that I'm wanting*
>   *So much as just finding the gold.*
> *It's the great, big, broad land 'way up yonder,*
>   *It's the forests where silence has lease;*
> *It's the beauty that thrills me with wonder,*
>   *It's the stillness that fills me with peace.*

Lou never mentioned it. When Steve finally asked, Lou said he
didn't think he'd like gold mining. "Not even the way the poem
made it sound? Wasn't that exciting?" The line went quiet. Steve
listened to the pause, thinking this might be a turning point.

Suddenly Lou blurted, "Robert Service was a hack!" The
conversation ended shortly after. Lou was impenetrable. You
could try to reach him through his own interests and he'd still

rebuff you.

If they were truly headed into a different time, maybe Lou would've been better off born into this new era: people cared more about tending to their feelings than about discovering what was achievable through hard work and determination. He raised the idea to Trudy. "Lou should've been a millennial," he said.

"What? How's that?" she asked. "Have you been listening to anything I just said?"

He had not, which was a slip up, but he had to get this out: "Cuz he's sensitive and helpless. Would rather be a victim than figure himself out."

"Woah, harsh!" Trudy said. "For a guy who doesn't like to talk about the past, you sure spend a lot of time dogging on Lou."

"What about it?" he snapped. Though really, he wanted to know.

"Lou's life probably didn't turn out how he wanted. There's probably a reason."

"Oh really? So what are we supposed to do? Drop everything? Orchestrate our lives around fixing his?" Steve couldn't tell where the anger came from, only that it was there.

"I think it's sort of like my sister," Trudy said, obviously referring to the one in Palmer, now on her fourth marriage. She rested her fingers on his wrist. "Our parents split right after I finished high school. She had three more years, and then money was a lot tighter. Betty got married the week after graduation. She made one mistake after another."

It felt like a scold even though Trudy's voice was soft. He folded his arms and tucked his fists into his armpits. He didn't like what she'd said and decided he'd drive her back to her own place after dinner, even though it was her weekend off from her kid. "I don't care what happened when," Steve said. "At some point, everybody needs to bear up and take responsibility for their own life."

"I'm not saying any different," Trudy said. "But sometimes things just don't work out."

Steve pushed back on the table. It was all too heavy for him. He should've just shown Rhonda his gold rather than ruin happy hour with all this. He hated how Lou made it impossible for him to enjoy himself. Steve's phone rattled by his glass. The name on the screen must've put dread in his eyes.

"What?" Trudy said. "Is it him?"

"No, it's Janine." He left the table to answer. There was no good reason for Janine to call now. "Yeah?" Steve maneuvered between the tables, past Rhonda laughing with a couple of suits.

"Got in an hour ago." Janine said. "Found him in his bathtub with a kitchen knife."

"Oh, Christ." Steve felt a weight drop through him like an anchor scraping bottom. The sequence of events immutable: one moment he's making a joke of Lou, next, this.

"He's alive for now. Lots of blood though."

"Should I catch a plane?"

"I don't think it's necessary. Not yet, anyways."

They hung up. Steve walked toward the entry. He had to push through a glut of Japanese tourists in the foyer, aiming their telephotos at the king crab shell mounted in glass behind the hostess' stand. That's all the state was now, something to take a picture of.

Outside, the smell of wet asphalt grazed the back of his throat. He didn't want to get in the van, didn't want to be anywhere. He stumbled past the cars toward the uncleared strip of land between the road and restaurant, like an animal seeking cover. He walked into the trees, footsteps crunching on dead leaves and sticks. The woods were indifferent to anything he'd done wrong. Shrouded in trees, he could imagine all the clocks stopped. He could see Lou running down the beach amidst the wreckage, his green glass float sparkling between his hands. But the clocks hadn't stopped. Time curved away from him. He should have done more to keep Lou tethered to this world. Not more, but something different. What?

Steve saw the sharp angles of adjacent office buildings poking above the birch branches. The pungent sweetness of tall grass and devil's club clung to him. He looked down and saw a tremendous rhubarb at his feet. Beneath flouncing leaves, big stalks splayed like arteries, blood-hued, bursting from the dirt. He took the tin from his pocket. He'd never tell anyone about his secret tribute, paid to whatever spirit might keep his brother alive. He popped open the lid. He sent his gold scattering into the undergrowth with one big breath.

LESLIE JONES was born and raised in Anchorage, Alaska. Her stories have also appeared in Narrative, The Baltimore Review, Necessary Fiction, and Day One. She received her MFA from Rutgers-Newark and lives in Brooklyn.

Little Men

Matthew Sullivan

The day that Lois found the Little Man—clinging to a spiraling leaf, screaming, falling, naked—she'd just rushed away from Alan's baseball practice to smoke an urgent cigarette. The Little Man had dropped from the hidden heights of an old oak and landed, lucky for him, on the soft top of her sandaled foot.

Not five minutes before the Little Man's fall, Lois had been standing in the dust of the little league diamond as Alan's coach passed a small white towel, just covered with blood, back and forth between his hands. Nearby a few cleated boys spat the husks of sunflower seeds to the dirt, and an anxious mother pressed ice against the bleeding boy's mouth. The coach tried his best to appear level-headed as he explained what Alan had done to his teammate, but Lois could see in the twitch and spit of his moustache that he was having a very hard time not spilling into rage. She couldn't blame him: the whole time Alan just stood there—gnawing on a wad of gum, fiddling with his elastic waistband—and offered no shock, no apology, nothing but his dumb-faced silence. In that moment Lois herself was so ashamed of her son that she couldn't stand to be there for even a second longer, so she turned and walked away, palms slapping the air, as everyone in the field watched her vanishing back.

She crossed the park and stopped to catch her breath on a sidewalk near the church. She took the Lucky Strikes tin out of her purse and lit a cigarette, and the rush of her first puff made the dandelions in the grass burn like stars. That was when it happened: the Little Man plunged past her sight, dragging with him a deep-green leaf—a parachute, of sorts—and bounced off the top of her foot. He was no bigger than a salt shaker.

Startled, Lois flicked her toes and the Little Man tumbled, still gripping his leaf. A stitch of guilt tightened in her gut. She plucked up the Little Man by his leaf and studied him hanging there, inches from her nose. His little hands clung to the stem, causing it to droop, and his little legs kicked in terror. His screams were horribly faint—but horrible nonetheless—and Lois's first reaction was not to hold him gently in her palm, nor to pop his balding skull between her fingers, but rather to stare up the rippled length of the tree and conclude, quite confidently, that the Little Man had not fallen, but jumped.

*   *   *

Four decades later, Lois sat at her kitchen table with a red gingham napkin pressed flat before her. Resting upon the napkin was an old Lucky Strikes tin spotted with rust, and alongside it, the Little Man's corpse.

In the next room she could hear Howard's voice muffled within his oxygen mask: "Alan's here tomorrow, right?"

"That sounds right," she said, but in truth she wasn't sure what Howard was referring to. *Alan's here tomorrow*: that did sound right somehow, and she was grateful that Howard had reminded her: their son Alan was coming to visit, wasn't he? She should get some meat out of the freezer, a nice roast or pork loin, and bake a pineapple upside-down cake. And she should really write these things down. She'd just had too much on her mind lately—what with rediscovering the Little Man and all.

"Alan calls you let me answer it," Howard said.

"Pork loin okay?"

Howard grunted and the television popped channel to channel, loud enough to raise the dead. Poor Howard: here but nowhere near, a victim of his years. Sometimes it was as simple as trying to reheat a bowl of chili in the freezer or blackening a pan with forgotten eggs, but sometimes it was worse, like the morning last week when she'd stepped out to the mailbox and found him on the floorboards of his old Ford pick-up, fiddling with the AM radio, a terrified panic in his eyes. His knuckles were bleeding and his pants were balled in the driveway and his penis hung out the side of his underwear like a turtle abandoning its shell.

"Just a bit of confusion," she'd said, leading him inside by the elbow.

Such pathetic incidents almost made Howard lovable again. But not quite. Even now, with his sneaky weenie locked inside an adult diaper, she couldn't help but recall the man's decades of deceit—which was why Lois, not one hour ago, had suspected that he'd been washing down his prescriptions with Gilbey's Gin again, hence her occasion to slam the stepstool against the fridge and probe the stale depths of the Libations Cupboard. Under inspection she found the liquor above the fridge as neglected as ever, positively fuzzed with dust, which meant that Howard had not been sneaking booze after all. But Lois was on a blaming crusade and would not allow this fact to settle just yet. So instead of closing up the cupboard she fished behind the bottles and found a deck of nudie playing cards (his), a vial of Valium (hers), an unopened fondue kit (theirs)—and a rusted Lucky Strikes tin, complete with the fragmented memory of what it contained: the Little Man.

That is, the Little Man's corpse.

And now at the kitchen table, with Howard snoring in the TV room, dark drapes drawn, Lois corrected the flow of her thoughts: of course there had been no Little Man. She must have seen him in a movie, *Darby O'Gill* or some puckeyrub, and transposed him into her liquor cabinet. But then what was this? Because here on the gingham napkin was the shriveled remains of something *organic*. The Little Man had become after all these years a blackened peel, a moldered husk, a knot of ancient bacon. She held him first with a fondue fork, tines beneath his armpits, then tenderly across her palm, like a child holding a hollow withered bird.

She tried to remind herself to get something out of the freezer for Alan's visit tomorrow, but the task was replaced with the certainty that yes, there indeed *had* been a Little Man, and falling into this memory was like pinching closed her nose and tipping backward off a boat.

*   *   *

"You gonna tell Dad?" The stoplight was red through Lois's station wagon windshield. "Are you gonna tell *Dad*?" Alan repeated, more desperate this time. "About what I done at baseball practice."

She looked in the rearview and saw him in the back seat, her eleven-year-old son. Now that they'd left the punched gloves and cracked bats of the ballfield, his baseball hat looked cheap and his practice jersey, spotted with blood, made her stomach turn. The poor kid's nose turned up so much that his nostrils were always in full view, and lately he'd had a cold so they were crusty and yellow. His natural look was so piggish that it felt normal to want to look away from him. Plus he smelled like rotting bread dough, her only child.

"It's what you *did*, Alan, not what you *done*."

"You gonna tell Dad what I *did* then?"

Lois popped in the car lighter and pulled her bursting purse into her lap. She really needed to clean it out: hairbrush, half packs of gum, a dozen empty matchbooks. Finally, her tin of Lucky Strikes. The light turned green.

"So, you gonna tell Dad?"

"I don't know." The truth was she was having a hard time processing exactly what Alan's coach had told her. Some boy needed stitches on his lips and tongue, she remembered, and probably a few caps on his teeth. Of course it was Alan's fault— it was always Alan's fault. And she remembered the coach's hands being sticky with blood as he spoke to her, so she could imagine him running across the playing field, snatching the bat out of Alan's grip and tossing it to the side, then getting right in there with his fingers to inspect the teammate's mouth and try to slow the bleeding and save what was left of his teeth. No wonder she'd bolted from the scene.

"Coach says I can't come back to practice until the doctor okays his mouth," he said. "And I gotta pay for his new glove because that one got bleedy."

"And *apologize*, Alan."

"And apologize," he said, drawing out his vowels.

She'd gotten pretty good at snapping open the Lucky Strikes tin with one hand while she was driving, but now she was having a heck of a time getting a cigarette out. She'd gotten her fingers inside, but the tin felt empty—no, not exactly empty. Just empty of cigarettes. But something was there, soft and fleshy like a pair of crossed fingers. She pinched at it and it pinched right back.

A tiny scream stabbed through the car and the car immediately swerved. A driver in the next lane honked. She squeezed the tin shut. The scream went mute as she threw her purse out of her lap to the floorboards.

"Mom?"

She looked up and Alan was there in the rearview, her ugly son, waiting for her response.

"I need to stop for smokes," she said.

*   *   *

Under the floral wallpaper of her kitchen, Lois closed her eyes and opened them again to find the Little Man's corpse was still there, sprawled on the table, on his gingham cloth. She leaned forward and sniffed and he still smelled like a man, all hay and semen, just as he had back when she'd found him.

She recalled the time when Alan was in junior high and she'd caught him smoking dried banana peels through a toilet paper roll cupped with aluminum foil—so maybe this was just some old homemade narcotic. Or maybe this was one of Alan's old action figures because when the boy was in kindergarten, she had to treat his Adventure People like they were living things. Their plastic faces were forever caked with applesauce, their chests plastered with Band-Aids. It all seemed very innocent, until the day he began using the hides of dead mice to fashion barbaric little cloaks and hooded masks for them—puckered specks where their eyes had been, tails as dry as twine—a discovery that caused her to contemplate calling the pastor or pediatrician. But then Howard came home from work and pointed out that the boy had probably just found a few old traps out in the garage that had long since snapped. It was the kind of thing that boys do, he explained, like catching a fish just to beat its head in with a rock. Lois didn't argue with him, but she never felt settled about the matter, especially in later years when she'd periodically find these same action figures burnt to a crisp in the garden or ripped of their limbs and buried in the yard, as if Alan's next step after outfitting them had been full-fledged torture.

So maybe this dead Little Man was one of those.

Lois placed the Little Man into his tin and dropped it into her bathrobe pocket and went to wake up Howard. Alan was going to be here tomorrow—wasn't he?—and the last thing she needed was to be wandering around the house with a shrunken little corpse in her grip for crying out loud.

*   *   *

From her seat in the station wagon Lois watched Alan shuffle through the parking lot toward the convenience store, his jersey still spotty with his teammate's blood. The elderly gentleman who ran the shop didn't mind her sending her young son in to buy her cigarettes, and today she was glad for it: she wanted Alan out of the car. At least long enough for her to take another peek.

With Alan inside the shop, she popped open the tin and allowed her gaze to fall upon the Little Man. He lay on his side, resting his head against his elbow, but at the lifting of the lid he stood and blinked and stretched. The slightest squeak escaped from his yawn.

He seemed exhausted, the Little Man. Or just plain lazy.

Sizing him up, Lois was surprised by her own disappointment. Though she'd seen him less than an hour ago, when she'd scooped him up after his leap from the tree, for some reason she expected that upon closer inspection the Little Man would reveal himself to be bearded with enlarged feet and pointy ears—the type of Little Man who'd feel right at home in a burlap cloak, holding aloft a wizard's staff. She wanted him to be elfin and otherworldly, a shrunken sage who'd share with her all the Wisdom of the World, but there in the tin, with stray specks of tobacco clinging to his damp skin and a tiny blemish on his rump, the Little Man could have been *any* little man: sunken chest, flabby belly, hairy groin. Lois stared at his penis, a fleshy little maggot. Its sight made her clench her teeth. The Little Man must have sensed her frustration because he dropped to his knees and covered his face with his hands. She thought she heard him crying.

Lois felt her spirits sink, but these feelings went away when the Little Man's little finger emerged from his pile and began jabbing at the sky:

Up. Up. Up.

When Lois looked up an alarming warmth rinsed through her. Alan was coming back to the station wagon, her carton of cigarettes beneath his arm, appearing for a moment much older than he actually was. For just a second there in the sunlight, the spots of blood on his uniform looked freshly spattered and his ball cap cast shadows across his face, and Lois had a vision of her young son as a grown man: wearing a thick moustache, cradling a paper sack of money under his arm, emerging from a liquor store he'd just robbed, its owner bleeding on the floor inside. She heard herself gasp and her fingers grabbed her lips. Alan smirked at her through the windshield—he was just a boy now, running a sunset errand for his mother—but *my god*, she thought, where do these thoughts come from? He's just a *boy*.

Lois was awash with fear and shame when from the bottom of her vision she caught the Little Man gesturing wildly in his tin, still naked, still pointing: *Up! Up!* She looked at Alan's moping form—he was almost to the car now, doing something weird with his tongue—and then she looked past him and realized what all the gesturing was about: right there, parked in front of the hot-sheet motel across the street, was Howard's unmistakable gray sedan.

*   *   *

Maybe she was simply remembering a caterpillar, she told herself as Howard's snores seeped through the house like a possession. Because caterpillars cling to leaves and fall from trees and a group of them teeming together inside a tin might make a juicy stick man.

*   *   *

There was Howard's unmistakable gray sedan, and not fifty feet away from the motel lobby, bordered by a splintery fence, was a bus stop where hookers—*Hookers!*—casually clustered.

Lois snapped the tin's lid shut as Alan climbed into the car.

"All set?" she said, mouth dry. But Alan just dropped the smokes over the seat.

Pulling out of the lot, she glanced again at Howard's car and wondered which of the long line of dreary motel rooms he was presently in, and she imagined at that very moment he was dropping his polyester slacks into a pile on the greasy rug and unbuttoning the dress shirt she'd been so careful to iron a few days back. He was supposed to be out-of-town all week, across the country selling industrial kitchen equipment to a representative from the US Army, but here was his sedan, parked at the seediest motel in the city, the most *natural* car in the lot, the car that *belonged* here the most, collecting sunshine and dust while she was rushing to pick up Alan from practice and make it to the bank and the butcher, not to mention tonight's PTA meeting—so when Howard called her later that evening to complain about the so-called tribulations of his so-called sales figures, and the so-called flight delays and so-called plumbing problems in the so-called airport hotel in so-called Maryland, all she could do was listen to his complaints and quietly envision his penis slithering into the mouth of a dirty, dirty woman.

She failed to tell him about finding the Little Man.

*   *   *

In the morning Lois and Howard awakened with the sun and swallowed trains of medication and spoons of sticky Cream of Wheat. They left cups of peach juice warming on the porch and knelt together in the garden. As Lois sprinkled a carton of mail-ordered ladybugs through the perennials, Howard pulled slugs from the soil and squished them between his fingers. At one time he and Lois had killed slugs with cans of beer and salty tonics, but this solution—bisecting them with a well-placed thumbnail—seemed just as effective and twice as fulfilling.

As if to validate what she was about to say, Lois tapped the pocket of her gardening apron, which perfectly fit the dented tin, which perfectly fit the dead Little Man. All morning she'd been feeling an inexplicable hunger to be close to him.

"Do you remember," she said, "when I found that little guy?"

Howard looked at her but his sight seemed to molder beneath the roots of his mind. A clear hose tethered to a small oxygen tank disappeared into his nostrils.

"Three, four inches," she added. "When Alan was in baseball."

"And this little guy was alive?"

Lois coughed to herself. "I think so. He didn't die until later, I think." She watched Howard for any adverse reaction, but his hands clawed through the soil like a diggitty mole and otherwise he appeared to have no reaction at all. "I may have even killed him."

Lois didn't know why she said this; she honestly didn't know if she had. Killed him, that is. She looked nervously at her watch. Howard used to help her sort such things out, but the two of them didn't exactly have the most logical conversations these days. It was more like a perpetual game of Name That Delusion, with Howard playing the smarmy host who liked to reach around and fondle the contestant ladies' asses with his eight tentacled arms.

For comfort, Howard had been kneeling on the floor mat of an old Buick and he took the opportunity to toss the mat to a different part of the garden and crawl that way.

"Isn't Alan coming today?" he said.

*   *   *

The last time Alan had visited his childhood home was well over a decade ago, when he was in his late thirties. He'd pulled his battered van into the driveway, unannounced, one November Saturday shortly after Howard's retirement. Howard and Lois had been raking leaves at the time and when Alan stepped out of the van they jumped out of their gloves to welcome him. Lois felt her hands trembling as she held him, and when she looked over and spotted Howard biting his lower lip to contain himself she started weeping.

"Mom, don't. C'mon, just don't."

Behind Alan the sky was gray and threatening rain. Holding his bony shoulders at arm's length it became clear to Lois just how *eroded* he'd become in the years since he'd left home. His ballcap was tilted at an odd angle and below it his long, gray hair clung to his unshaven neck. When he grinned through a bristly goat's beard Lois noticed that his front teeth were beige and slightly chipped, but before she could ask when he'd last had a check-up Alan waved his hands and announced that they should brace themselves: he had something Big to share.

"Meet my bride," he said, then turned his head toward the van and shouted, "Elise!"

Lois did everything she could to appear happy for her errant son but her tongue felt swollen and she could barely swallow. As far as she knew, Alan had not had a second date, let alone a girlfriend, since eighth grade. Apparently things had changed, she thought, as she watched Alan's new wife emerge from the van and bounce up the driveway. Lois dug her fingernails into Howard's forearm when it became clear that Elise was half his age.

"I told you they'd freak," Alan said.

"Only cause you're a cradle-robbing son of a bitch!" Elise said, swaying into his side with a crash. Alan crashed back and giggled.

"Alan, really," Howard said, "it's just great."

Howard mumbled his congratulations, making excuses for their stilted reaction, but Lois just stood there, attempting to hide the blanket of dread that had settled over her. Elise's face was muddy with make-up and downright *festooned* with platinum hair. Below the chin she was all turquoise and boobs, and for a moment Lois thought she may have been one of those Russian brides sad men get. When she asked Elise if that was where she was from she felt immediately foolish.

"Russia?" Elise said, slapping at her hip. "Oh no, Mama—Alan saved me from a Dairy Queen in Lubbock!"

*   *   *

For the first few days, way back when he was alive, the Little Man had lived in Lois's purse, cradled inside of her Lucky Strikes tin, but it wasn't long before she'd made a little home for him inside an old JC Penny's shoebox that she kept stashed beneath her bed. Howard was theoretically still away on business, and late at night, while Alan dozed beneath baseball wallpaper with his hands down the front of his pajamas—even boys were men—Lois poked holes in the top of the box and sprinkled cotton balls in there for cushions. For food she raked hot dogs and iceberg lettuce through a cheese grater, and the occasional drip of honey or marmalade on a tidbit of bread crust. When she placed a ceramic thimble of water in the corner of the box, the Little Man leapt up from his cottony lounge and urinated into it, a long steady stream that splashed the wall of the box, as if he'd been holding his pee for days. Sometimes he seemed to shiver with a chill, but when she tried to get him to crawl into an old infant's sock that she'd fashioned into a mu-mu he refused, preferring instead to go nude, often with his fists planted on his hips. Whenever she left the house, the Little Man flopped willingly into his cigarette tin, and Lois couldn't help but wonder if he found comfort in simply being close to her.

Lois tried to convince herself that the Little Man was a secret pleasure in her life, but there was no accounting for the fact that he spent so much time *crying*. This was the one certainty: the Little Man's little misery. Sure, he'd quiet down while nibbling on a bit of orange pulp or when he slurped grape soda straight from the bottlecap, but it was never long before the crying came again. His tears would subside when she gave him her undivided attention, such as when she bathed him gently in a teacup of warm water, or allowed him to run laps around the kitchen table as she cheered him on. But as soon as she began to wrap things up, he'd drag his feet like a whipped schoolboy and sit solemnly on the table's edge, kicking his naked legs over the side and crying into his hands.

She tried sometimes to talk to him but it never went anywhere:

"Do you want to go back to your tree—is that it?"

—

"Would you like me to leave you in the garden? I could give you something to defend yourself with. Needles and toothpicks, like in kids' books. Would you like that?"

—

"I could give you many peas."

In response he always cried harder. At first his crying had left Lois wishing she could take on his pain, accept it as her own, but as it escalated she simply grew frustrated and a growing part of her wanted to crush the Little Man and end all this nonsense. She could pretend to want to show him something in a book, then slam it shut, or bait a mouse trap with a chocolate chip and *snap*!

Sometimes she imagined she was him, looking up at a big, powerful Her.

*   *   *

When Lois looked up from her spot in the garden Howard was on the porch, untangling the thin tube of his oxygen tank, and a young man was striding across their lawn, waving Hello. Last winter the furnace guy sat down for a cup of coffee before changing out the filters, and with Howard's condition there'd been a few home medical visits, but otherwise Lois was hard pressed to recall a genuine visitor lately. Which was why she was so excited when Howard reminded her that Alan would be here tonight.

Lois immediately suspected that the approaching young man belonged to some kind of pushy religion, the kind where all the males had parted hair and looked like the dentist on the old Rudolph show. He was a tricky little bugger, too: before she could even begin to stand up the young man was on the porch, clapping Howard's back and rocking his heels on a creaky board. She could hear him speaking to Howard, something about how we should keep tabs on our eternal lives just as we keep tabs on the lives of our vehicles. Take for instance that pick-up truck parked in the driveway. Was that a '62 Ford? It was. Might he take a look? He might.

Lois had had enough of his righteous malarkey and would've chased the young man away with a garden rake had he not been so darned attentive to Howard. Usually people took one look at the man's blank gaze and turned their attention to Lois, so she found it refreshing for the young man to be so warm to her husband. Howard, for his part, was excited enough to go inside and rummage for a photograph of the pick-up truck on the day he'd purchased it half-a-century earlier. And while he was inside, the young man took the opportunity to pull Lois to the side of the porch.

"You do know why I'm here, don't you?" he said.

Lois stared deeply into the young man's eyes—brown, honest—but didn't think she recognized him.

"Is it about Alan?" she whispered.

*   *   *

Lois was proud of herself as she followed Alan and Elise through their dim apartment, holding with both hands a cling-wrapped bowl of grasshopper mousse. In order to buy the bottle of crème de menthe that the recipe required, she'd had to overspend the grocery budget, but she was glad to have done so. After all, welcoming newlyweds home from their honeymoon was a special occasion—not the time to be pinching pennies.

When she set the mousse on the kitchen counter Elise clapped and peeled back its cling wrap. Then she plunged her finger straight into the green fluff and held it out to Alan, who slurped the mousse right from her fingertip.

"You dirty *dog*," Elise said, hissing.

Lois mumbled something about *leaving you lovebirds alone*, then went roaming through the apartment in search of Howard, who had somehow disappeared between the car and the apartment. He was nowhere to be found, and after dipping her head into the living room and bedrooms she rounded the corner and somehow walked straight back into the kitchen again. She stopped quietly in the doorway and caught Alan and Elise sharply elbowing each other as they arranged a platter of cold cuts. They looked like children playing house, Lois thought, until Alan shot out his hand and *twisted* Elise's nipple—roughly, not knowing that his mother could see the whole scene—*twisted* as if to correct the girl's behavior, and *my god*, the look on her son's face!

An awful chill rushed up Lois's spine. She stumbled to the

living room couch and put her head between her knees. When she lifted her head again, Howard was kneeling by the television, scooping up an ashtray of butts and paper matches that he'd somehow spilled.

"When's dinner?" he said.

Lois ignored him. She could only hold her cheeks and hope that the dread she'd just felt had been terribly, terribly misleading. Alan wasn't capable of *that*, was he? But she knew. Even then she knew. Maybe she couldn't yet isolate the toaster cord or the coring knife or the meat thermometer he'd use to finish her off, but she felt it al lright: Elise's certain murder, hovering in the air, as if the act was haunting that apartment years before she'd even died.

*   *   *

"It is about Alan, actually," the wholesome young man said.

Lois felt hot, as if leaning over a canning pot. She held on to the porch's railing and listened to Howard rummaging somewhere in the house.

"Alan doesn't live here anymore," she said.

"I know. I've been visiting him down in Livingston." The young man gestured toward the porch swing. "Would you like to sit down?"

"I'm fine right here," Lois said.

The young man reached over and picked off a leaf from a creeping grape vine.

"I'm sorry to just show up like this. It's just become rather desperate."

Lois was confused. She tapped her fingertips on the hidden tin sitting perfectly in her apron. Somehow its presence comforted her.

"Did you say you're from Livingston?" she said.

"I can see the prison from my church," he said. "I visit some of the men there. Alan being one."

"Go on."

"I came a long way to speak to you," he said. "You do know what today is, don't you? You do understand what happens tonight at midnight?"

"It's Alan's big day, isn't it?"

"Tonight he sits in the chair."

"I see," she said, nodding.

"The electric chair? Do you understand what I'm saying? No stays, no appeals. Alan is going to die tonight."

"Yes," she said, "I see."

"I'm surprised there aren't any reporters," he said, looking up and down the block. "You might watch for them later. Plan to stay inside. Close the curtains if you have to."

"We always do. It saves on the cooling."

"Listen," the young man said, leaning toward her, "this is important. Alan is going to call you beforehand. He needs you to pick up the phone."

"We've been unplugging the phone lately."

"I'm aware of that," he said. "It's why I drove all the way up here. He needs to hear your voice tonight. Will you answer when he calls?"

"You came all the way here," Lois said, "to ask me to answer the phone?"

"In a nutshell, yes. You need to pick up when it rings tonight."

"Is that everything, then?"

The young man made his way off the porch, holding just a stem, walking away.

"After tonight, there won't be another chance," he said.

*　　*　　*

The iron hissed and coughed in Lois's grip as she stroked it over Howard's work shirts. Howard, fresh from his so-called trip to Maryland, was in the shower down the hall, shaving in the steam, taking his time, and Alan was downstairs watching Saturday morning cartoons and cramming his spent candy wrappers between the couch cushions. And then there was the Little Man: perched on the quilted edge of the ironing board, rocking gently back and forth as Lois clacked the cone of the iron between plastic buttons, straightening cotton, straightening cotton. He was completely nude and crying, as usual, into his little hands.

A few minutes ago, as Howard was dumping his travel clothes

out of his suitcase for Lois to wash, she could faintly hear the Little Man beneath the bed, scratching at the inside of his shoe-box. When Howard disappeared to take a shower—to wash off a week of hooker crust—Lois felt her annoyance growing.

"This really needs to stop," she hissed into the shoe box. "You can come out for five minutes and that's *all*."

She held her palm out next to the box and the Little Man climbed on, holding her thumb tightly as she crossed the room. A moment later he hopped from her fingertips to the ironing board, found his seat and began to weep.

"What on earth do you have to cry about, anyway? What is it you *want*?"

And that was when The Little Man, dangling his skinny little legs over the edge of the ironing board, wiped his tears and held out his hands. At first Lois didn't understand what he was gesturing. He opened his palms—pale little snowflakes—and his eyes met hers for just long enough to see the desire they contained.

You, he pointed. *You! You! You!*

"This is *ridiculous*," she hissed, and set about ironing Howard's shirt collar with a fierceness that nearly sent the Little Man flying off his perch. But she couldn't help herself—he wanted *her*—and for the briefest instant she imagined sitting in the back of a Greyhound bus with the shoebox in her lap, cutting across the country beneath giant Midwestern stars, lifting the lid in the dark to sprinkle cookie crumbs into her Little Man's lap.

You!

Howard's shower went quiet down the hall and Alan's cartoons paused downstairs.

And then Lois brought the iron down right on top of him, the Little Man, pinning him against the edge of the ironing board, and pressed, pressed, pressed—first with her arm, then with the full weight of her body, rocking the iron bow to stern until his squealing became hissing and the hissing bubbled to a stop.

She blew a stray hair out of her eyes. She lifted the iron to examine the smoking effigy caked against its soleplate, looking like a sticky blackened root, and she just had time to shake it into the pile of laundry at her feet when Howard entered the room, naked except for a towel, pausing to look at her as he dug a Q-tip deep into the waxy recess of his ear. Alan entered next, as if on cue, still wearing his pajamas and scratching at his nose.

The pair of them stared at her, expectant.

"You got something cooking?" Alan said, tilting his nose into the air.

*   *   *

At the dinner table, an empty setting filled the space between Lois and Howard—a blank white plate, a hollow glass, a folded napkin weighed down by a fork and a knife. Howard had set the table while Lois was finishing mashing the potatoes and when she carried the food in she didn't have the heart to comment on that third empty setting. So the two of them ate their dinner in silence until midway through Howard's pile of pork.

"Isn't it tonight Alan's coming?" he said.

Lois touched the back of his hand. "Maybe we got the date wrong," she said.

She could sense circuits overheating behind her husband's face. He looked down his nose at her, forking the empty air. "You need to get a calendar," he said.

"I know, dear."

Howard tucked back into his plate, and when he finished, he drowned his uncertainty in the blare of the television while Lois cleared the table and washed the dishes. She took her time, drying each dish with a tea towel, and later, dawdling through her coupons. When Howard's snores finally began to boomerang through the house, she pulled the Little Man's tin out from her apron and spread out his shriveled corpse, for the second night in a row, on the gingham napkin. Then she shuffled into the living room and muted the television. Howard didn't budge, so she leaned over the side table next to him and lifted the old phone from its cradle. It was silent inside. The end of the cord made a satisfying *click* as she plugged it into the wall jack.

Then Lois waited in the kitchen, turning the Little Man this way and that. From her spot she could just see the phone next to Howard and she wondered if it would really ring tonight, as the young man earlier had promised. She couldn't recall exactly *when* she and Howard had decided to begin unplugging the phone for long stretches at a time, but she did remember how decisive the initial choice had felt. It was the photos that did it, if she remembered right. The prosecution had matted them on posterboard and propped them on tripods for the jury to see: Elise, hogtied with a toaster cord on the kitchen table, naked and swollen and unnaturally bent; the coring knife sticking out from under her shoulder blade, as if Alan had been trying to shimmy it off; the meat thermometer buried in her temple, surrounded by all that platinum hair.

Lois squeezed shut her eyes and when she opened them again she decided it would be a good idea to put the Little Man's corpse back into the Libations Cupboard until morning, just in case Howard woke up and began snooping about, as he sometimes did. So she scooped up the Little Man and pushed the stepstool over and climbed one, two, three rungs to the top.

Shortly after the photos of Elise's body had been introduced as evidence, Lois and Howard left the courtroom—holding hands, their heads down, ignoring the flashes of photographers— and walked straight past the cafeteria and out to the meters where they'd parked. On the drive home neither said a word, but that night they turned on the local news and squeezed close to each other on the couch.

Lois reached deep inside the Libations Cupboard, past the dusty bottles, holding the corpse gently in her fist as if he was a gecko or a budgie. She was about to drop the Little Man into the hidden grime behind when the ringing phone sent a jolt through the house. It had been so long since she'd heard the sound that the stepstool shifted and creaked beneath her and she nearly teetered right off the top. Her hand bumped the bottles and they gonged like bells. Howard snarfled for a second then went back to his snores. Lois stared at the phone, frozen in the moment, half regretting her decision to plug it in. It rang again and again.

She knew she'd have time to answer it if she could just unfreeze and climb down and snatch it out of its cradle. And she was about to—she really was—when she felt a faint tickle coming from the lumpy mass in her hand: a trace of tiny fingernails, scratching for her attention.

MATTHEW SULLIVAN'S *debut novel, Midnight at the Bright Ideas Bookstore, was published this summer by Scribner. His short stories have been awarded the Robert Olen Butler Fiction Prize and the Florida Review Editor's Prize, and have appeared in Joyland, The Chattahoochee Review, Fugue and other places. He received his M.F.A. from the University of Idaho, and he currently teaches writing and literature at Big Bend Community College in rural Washington State.*

www.matthewjsullivan.com

Out of Our Suffering

Kasey Thornton

Yesterday Ms. Atkins handed out "The Cask of Amontillado" during literature time. She said the principal said the story was too hard for fifth graders but that no child should go to middle school not knowing what bullying means or how to handle it. By the end of the story I was not sure who was the bully or what the right way to handle bullying was but I knew I wanted to tie my daddy's hunting dog to a tree until she starved to death. Cole Tanner couldn't say Amontillado and kept saying armadillo and Ms. Atkins made him put his name on the board.

When I got home I ate supper like everything was normal and then I went to the shed. I tied a rope right around Loretta's neck since I've seen her slip out of her collar before. The two of us went way into the woods past the deer stand on the other side of Coolie's pond and I cow-knotted her to a good tree and walked away. She stood there watching me leave with a stupid look in her eyes.

This morning my eyes are glued shut with gunk. I am cleaning all the crumbled worksheets out of the bottom of my book bag on the porch when Daddy comes out of the shed and says "Where's Loretta?"

"I don't know. I went looking for her last night," I say.

"Probably chased a possum into the woods," he says and

lights a cigarette. He tells us all the time that he will never love anything as much as he loves that dog. She was one thousand and eleven dollars plus a hundred more for all her shots.

My stomach hurts on the bus but it's a different kind of pain than the kind that makes you throw up. It's like someone is poking around inside me with a knife. Ms. Atkins makes us pronounce the Latin part of "The Cask of Amontillado" over and over: *nemo me impune lacessit.* It means if someone hurts you, you should always hurt them back.

Mama is frying up liver pudding and eggs when I get home from school. We have breakfast for supper about three times a week but we don't get breakfast for breakfast except on Christmas so I don't mind. I hear the toaster pop so I know there won't be pancakes. Her foot catches on the plastic part of the floor that is bent up from the damp beneath our doublewide and she slams her head into a cabinet and says goddamn it.

She wouldn't have said it if Daddy was in the house or he'd tell the preacher on Sunday. Then we'd all have to stand on the porch of the church and listen to Pastor Ryan talk about what happens to people who don't give God the respect He deserves. One time he talked until even the choir ladies left.

Abigail is seven years older than me. She is the queen of the house or that's what she wants you to believe. She sits at the desk in her and Daddy's room and does homework until Mama goes in and tells her to come be social. Abigail never asks to have friends over so school is the only time she talks to anyone except for when she's going at me. One day she told me I was an accident and when I asked her what that meant she said never mind. I asked Mrs. Weston what it means to be an accident and her eyes got all sad and she said that it means I am a miracle.

Loretta is an outside dog so no one will worry too much about her tonight but I don't know how long it takes dogs to starve. I feel like if I went without food I'd die in a few hours but I like to eat. I am trying to get a body like Abigail's because she looks like a model in Daddy's white tank tops, all hips and tits since she got her period and he said that she was a woman now. That's why she gets to sleep in the big bed with him and I sleep on the couch. Hopefully Loretta will starve before long because all hell will bust loose if he figures out what I did. I go to my red chair in the living room and root around in my book bag for the Amontillado story to read before supper. We have to underline the words we don't know like *afflicted* and *grotesque* and *crypt* and look them up in a dictionary.

Mama comes in and starts fanning herself with her apron. She has been at the hospital where she works since four o'clock in the morning and she looks dog-tired. Daddy comes in wiping his hands on a rag. I ask him what *insufferable* means and point to the word on the paper. He goes behind my chair and reads what it says. "It's what hell is," he says. "Something so terrible you can't stand it for another minute. Like your Mama."

She looks at him but doesn't say anything. He gets that nastiness in his eyes and stares her down. Then he pokes his lip out like she's hurt his feelings. "See? She doesn't even talk to me. Acts like she's too good to talk to your sweet old pops," he says.

"She's a big fat bitch," I say.

Mama and Daddy hate each other but not the kind of hate you see on TV when the wife and husband fight over who is cooking supper and who is sleeping on which side of the bed and then they kiss and the audience laughs. It is not like that at all. One time my daddy used a vacuum cleaner like a baseball bat to beat the tar out of Mama and when she fell down all the dirt landed on her and she looked like a dead person partway buried. One time he threw his mug of hot coffee in her face and took Abigail into the bedroom and the two of them didn't come out for two days.

When they fight, it is like those cartoons where the ground is glue. I cannot move even to blink so I have to stand there and watch whatever happens. Abigail's legs work fine so she runs. When I told my Aunt in a letter that it makes me scared when they fight she wrote back and said, "Your daddy is a good man."

When he gets angry it feels like the whole house is on fire and the ground is going to swallow us right up because God will decide that we are too nasty to live on earth and hell is a better place for us. Loretta is probably laid down in a bed of leaves right now wondering when I am coming back to get her. Even though I did the right thing by tying her out there it feels like I'm the one who's dying instead.

Today everyone had ants in their pants after recess and Ms. Atkins yelled at Cole Tanner to sit down and shut up. When people yell I get sweaty and sometimes I pee my pants a little even if they're not even mad at me. My body can get scared of a thing even when my brain isn't scared of it at all and that is what I hate most about myself. My heart feels like a bird slamming into a window trying to get out even though I am cool as a cucumber. I raise my hand and say, "May I go see Mrs. Weston?" like I am supposed to and Ms. Atkins tells me to take the hall pass and go.

Mrs. Weston is my guidance counselor. She's got big hair like Dolly Parton and no lips. Her husband is Austin who owns the grill in town and if I go there and tell him I didn't get any lunch he'll give me a grilled cheese that is dripping with butter and that is my favorite. I think he probably knows I always get lunch but he gives me one anyway with this sad look on his face that a lot of people give me before they're about to do something special for me. I like when people are sad for me. I also like being in the hallway during class when I am the only one there and everyone else is trapped in their rooms doing flashcards or reading or multiplications. I feel like I am at a zoo watching the animals but I can do what I please.

The guidance office is yellow with chairs and a couch. There are paintings on the wall of flowers and fields with flowers in them and flowers in vases and people holding flowers and there are fresh flowers on the desk and on all the tables in the waiting area and it all reminds me of the funeral of the boy who died from his needles last year. There's a fish tank bubbling in the corner making a nice sound that would put me to sleep if I had time to lie down.

Mrs. Weston pokes her Dolly Parton head out of her office and I am not sweating and my heart is quiet but I don't want to tell her because she will make me go back to class. I have been seeing her since Abigail backhanded me at home and I got the bruise on my face and Ms. Atkins told the office that I was at risk.

Mrs. Weston holds up a laminated poster with a bunch of faces on it and asks how I'm feeling today. I point to the one with the angry eyes. She asks me what I'm angry about and I say that Ms. Atkins yelled at Cole Tanner.

"Do you think Cole Tanner deserved to be yelled at?"

"He's a shit."

"Where did you learn to call people shits?"

"Everyone calls people shits."

She leans forward in her seat. "Do your Mama and Daddy call each other shits?" I say no. "Do they call you a shit?" I say no. "What was it about Cole Tanner getting yelled at that made you angry?"

"I got sweaty and my heart got going and my stomach hurts."

"Can you point to where it hurts?"

I touch my belly button. This is what I do whenever any doctor asks me where my stomach hurts like I'm going to point to my knee or something. It is not a pain that comes and stays but when it comes it hurts bad enough to make my whole body go hard for a few seconds. She says uh-huh and writes something down.

"I am angry because my Mama is mean to my Daddy," my mouth says all of a sudden.

She looks at me over her glasses. "How is your Mama mean to your Daddy?"

"She looked really good before she got married. Skinny and pretty hair. But she let herself go after she had the kids and now she's a lazy fat ass and I can't stand to look at her much less touch her or have her in my bed."

Mrs. Weston says, "Emma, is that really how you feel about your Mama?"

"She is *insufferable*."

Mrs. Weston looks like I punched her straight in her mouth and I'm not sure if that is a good thing. She says that's enough for one day, but she will talk to Ms. Atkins to make sure it's okay if I come back next week.

When I'm in the hallway by myself I like to only step on the red tiles, or take the whites two at a time, or pretend the black ones are lava. I look in the windows at the other students and when they see me out by myself I give them a "haha" smile because I am clever enough to get out of class whenever I want and they are not. It is not so bad to be at risk.

When I get home Daddy is under Bobby Tanner's pickup. He

fixes trucks in our garage for money. Everyone else in the house is lazy and living on his hard work and he breaks his back to put food on our table and clothes on our asses and what thanks does he get? Mama told him a few weeks ago that her job as a nurse pays more bills than his did even when he had a job and let's just say no one talks about who has a job and who doesn't anymore.

Daddy shimmies out from under the truck where he's laying on a folded towel and says, "You seen Loretta today?" and I say, "No sir" and he grunts a little and rolls away again.

I need to wash my dirty panties. Mama's car isn't in the driveway and Abigail is reading at her desk eating a pack of fruit snacks so I know no one will see me. The pain in my stomach is bad but I don't know who I should tell. I decide to just let it work itself out. That is what my Mama says when there is a problem. "It'll work itself out."

Most people don't know what couches look like on the inside but I do because I sleep on the couch. If you lift up the cushions there are pockets and zippers where you can keep things and no one will ever find them. If Abigail makes Daddy mad he says he's going to put me in the bed with him and make her sleep on the couch and then she stops whatever she is doing to make him mad.

I don't mind not having a room for myself because the whole trailer is my room. Mama does my laundry and folds it and keeps it in stacks on the kitchen floor against the wall so I don't need a dresser or closet and everything else I have fits in the couch. I keep my McDonald's toys, my Barbie, my deck of cards, and my beaded jump rope under the right cushion and my World Book "C" encyclopedia and letters from my Gamma under the left one. I keep my messed up panties in grocery bags way in the back past the cushions until I can sneak them into the washing machine. I don't want anyone in the house to know I am in the fifth grade and I still pee my pants when I get scared, especially not Abigail who will make fun of me to no end to Daddy who will get mad at Mama for not teaching me any better even though she taught me good enough but I just can't help it sometimes.

There are four dirty panties in there since I last washed them. They smell to high heaven when I dump them into the machine and turn it on.

"You doing laundry?" Abigail says from Daddy's room.

"Do you hear the washing machine?" I say.

"Shut up you little shit."

I go to check on Loretta and she wags her tail and stands up. She is panting a lot but she's bouncing around tugging on the rope. I stay a few feet away from where she'd be able to jump on me. "Do you know my Daddy loves you more than he loves anything?" She swings her tail back and forth and goes down on her front legs like she wants to play and barks twice. She doesn't look hungry to me yet. Something wet happens between my legs even though I didn't feel myself pee at all.

When I walk back home I move my panties from the washer into the dryer. Mama is in her bedroom changing out of her work clothes but she hasn't checked the laundry yet. She's got stuff on the counter to make spaghetti with meat sauce and I hope there's butter toast and stinky cheese to go with it.

I go to the bathroom and pull my pants down and there is a chunk of blood in my panties about as long as my thumb. A few months ago Ms. Atkins took us to a health center and they separated the girls and boys and talked to us about boobs and vaginas so I know I am a woman now. The first person I want to tell is Abigail but I know she will say something that will make me mad. I root around in the kitchen cabinet for a grocery bag so I can put the bloody panties under the couch cushion until I can figure out what to do with them. Someone slams the trashcan lid shut behind me and scares me to death. When I turn around Abigail sees me holding a wad in my hand and comes towards me and I don't bother backing away. She peels open my fingers and sees the panties with blood on them and something comes over her. She hits me so hard that it feels like my head turns all the way around like an owl. My eyes start watering even though I am not sad but angry.

Abigail grabs the panties and wraps them in a grocery bag while I am still trying to stand then throws the bag into the trashcan. "Were you going to hide them in the couch like your piss-pants?" Her voice is nasty.

"Shut up," I say, scared.

She jerks me up by my arm and takes me into the bathroom

and closes the door. Abigail pushes me toward the toilet and roots around in the cabinet and pulls a white stick out of a box. I know it's a tampon and I know what tampons are for but I wasn't listening very hard the day Ms. Atkins explained how to use it because I thought maybe I would be special and not have to.

Abigail unwraps it and gives it to me. I stare at the little teeth at the end. "It won't hurt," she says. "You put the thick part in you and then push the thin part and it makes the thing come out."

It makes sense but it doesn't make me feel any better about sticking something like that up inside me. Abigail turns around and I take down my pants and sit down on the commode. I put the thing between my legs and wiggle it around but nothing happens. I push the thin part with my thumb and the whole thing falls into the toilet.

"Dumbass," Abigail says and fishes another one out of the box. "Try again. Don't push it until it's in."

"How do I know when it's in?"

"You'll know."

So I unwrap the new tampon and move it in circles until it finally finds the right place to slide in. Then I pull the plastic part out and Abigail turns around and takes it from me like she is not even holding something gross. She puts it back into the wrapper.

"See how I did that?" she says. "Then you wrap it in toilet paper, the same way you wrap your panties so no one can see what's inside."

"Okay," I said. When I bend down to pull my jeans back up, I can feel it thick and hard inside of me. It hurts.

"You gotta change it every six hours."

"Okay," I say.

"Don't tell anyone," she said, looking me in the eye. "Not Daddy or Mama."

"Okay."

"If you get your panties bloody throw them away."

"Okay."

"Give me a day or two to figure things out."

I don't know what she means but I say okay. She leaves me standing there sore between my legs with my cheek busted open from the dime-store ring on her hand.

We eat our spaghetti later in the living room. Mama sits on the floor and Abigail sits on the couch with Daddy and I sit in my armchair. Daddy finishes what's on his plate and sops up the sauce with his buttered toast then goes into the kitchen for seconds. Mama doesn't eat much and Abigail is picking at her food like a bird. Daddy and I are the fastest eaters in the house and we eat the most by far. Sometimes Mama jokes and says, "No one's going to take it from you."

"Y'all seen Loretta today?" Daddy asks from the kitchen.

"No sir," Abigail says. I stay quiet.

"We could call Dale," Mama says. "He'd help us look."

"Officer Overton?" Abigail asks.

"Yeah."

"He came to our school last week to do the drug talk," she says. Abigail stops eating and stares off like something very far away just became more interesting than what's sitting in front of her. I met Officer Overton a bunch of times around town and I remember Mama helping out with his wedding. I got to help clean up afterward and when we were done his new wife whose name I cannot remember let me keep a bunch of the fake flowers.

"I think someone stole her," Daddy says. "Good dog, purebred. Loretta was one thousand and eleven dollars. Plus a hundred more for all her shots." He has said this I know at least one thousand and eleven times. "If someone stole her I swear to God there'll be hell to pay."

"What if someone stole me or Abigail?" I am trying to get his mind off of Loretta so he doesn't get any ideas about going and looking for her.

"I'd kill anyone who tried to take my babies away from me. I'd kill them for even thinking about it. I don't care who it is."

Mama puts her fork down like she is full. I start thinking about all the ways my Daddy could kill someone. I think about poor Fortunato being walled up with bricks in a hole.

"Is being buried alive a bad way to die?" I say.

"I can't think of a worse way," Daddy says.

"What about getting shot?" I ask.

Mama sucks her teeth. "Emma Lynn, don't talk about people getting shot."

Daddy lets me shoot his Beretta in the woods and he says

Mama can't say anything about it. He taught me how to stand with my legs in a stance and how to cup my left hand under my right even if that is not how they do it in the movies.

"Getting shot is better," Daddy says. "At least you don't suffer."

I slurp my spaghetti and Abigail stares at me all mean and tells me to straighten up. She's always acting high and mighty like she doesn't have to care about anything or anyone in the house as long as Daddy treats her like a princess. Plus I can still feel the tampon in me and the cut on my face and they make me angry at her too.

"What about starving to death?" I say.

"You'd go thirsty first," Daddy says. He's still not looking up from his food. "But that's a sorry way to die too. Worse than being buried alive."

"So starving or going thirsty is the worst way to die," I say.

"Making something suffer is worse than putting something out of its misery," he says. "That's why hunters need to shoot straight or the deer suffers and you've got to walk up on it and pop it in its head."

"Pop it in its head," I say.

After dinner Abigail sits at the desk squinting at a piece of paper because Daddy won't let a computer in the house. She writes as fast as she can like she is a person in a movie trying to move a satellite or turn off a bomb, like the whole world depends on how fast she can write.

I go with a flashlight to see Loretta after everyone goes to bed. She barks when she sees me and she has pulled on her rope so hard that it is making her neck bleed. Her brown fur is matted with red and her eyes are watering like she's been crying even though I know that dogs don't cry. She's panting and yelping and whining. I think about the tampon inside of me drinking up blood and I think about what Officer Overton is doing right now in his brick house with his wife whose name I still cannot remember and maybe a kid too, like me, and I think about the ground opening up and somehow I know it's too late. I walk backward with my eye on Loretta until the flashlight beam can't find her anymore.

Abigail gives me four tampons before I get on the bus in the morning and tells me not to forget to change them. "Just get through today," she says, but I am not sure what will happen if I do or don't. When I can't hold my pee anymore I put a tampon in my sock and ask Ms. Atkins if I can go to the bathroom. I sit on the toilet and do the whole thing myself. I never knew why there were little trashcans in the stall until now but now I see that it's a good idea.

I get off of the bus and stop by Austin's and he throws a grilled cheese into the iron for me. My stomach feels emptied out but not like I'm hungry. The emptiness feels better than being full of food but I don't know why. When I get into my pajamas after dinner, my shoulders are as soft as Abigail's. I even have an easier time brushing my hair because it is shining at the top. Ms. Atkins said that periods can make some girls look ugly but some girls have a period and look even prettier than they did before. That must be what happened to Abigail and maybe even me. I stare at myself in the mirror and like what I see which is not something I'm used to. I bet I will look like a model in a few months if I keep having periods like this one. I stay in the bathroom for maybe an hour painting my fingernails red and my toenails purple. I even get Abigail's green mud stuff and slather it all over my face. I wait for it to get hard and then I wash it off. I can't tell if it has changed my face at all but it felt good to do it anyway and that's enough.

The lights are all out when I come out of the bathroom feeling pretty as I ever felt. I go toward the couch to get some beauty sleep but I hear Abigail and Daddy talking in their bedroom. It's hard for anyone but me to sneak around because I am still light enough not to make the floor creak and I know where to step and where not to. I crouch to hear and Abigail makes a noise like a whining dog. I've heard it before and tonight it is louder than normal and it sounds like she is crying for something like a fussy baby. The noise makes my face turn hot and my hands sweat and I feel like our whole house does not belong to the world anymore but to some other place where nothing good will ever happen to us again. It gets in me and swims around in my empty stomach and between my legs like a poison.

After a few minutes I hear my Daddy grunt a few times

and then he hollers out. He says fuck then neither of them say anything for a long time until he whispers something but I can't hear what it is. She says something back in a girly voice. He laughs and then they are quiet.

I don't turn the TV on when I lay down because I have a TV in my head tonight. I am a secret agent or a Power Ranger or a ninja assassin and I am not afraid of anything. If the ground opens to swallow us up I will flip out of the way and let my mama and daddy and Abigail get sucked down to hell and then I'll figure out how to get right with God again for my own damn self.

When the clock says 1:37 a.m. Abigail comes out of their room and I pretend to be asleep. She comes right up to the couch. "Get a bag and put some clothes in it. Be quiet."

"Why?"

"I said so."

"Why?"

She snatches me up to show she is serious. Her nails dig into my wrist but I don't squeal. Abigail drags me into the kitchen and pushes me toward my stacks of clothes, then grabs one of the cloth grocery bags that you take to the store yourself to save the earth.

"Fill it," she says. "Pants, shirts, panties. I got your toothbrush and some tampons." She goes to the closet and gets my coat while I do what she says. Then Abigail puts one hand on me and the other on the doorknob and she breathes out hard and opens the door. My whole body must be sweating because when the cold air hits the wet patches of my skin I start shaking. She closes the door as quietly as she can and gives me my coat. I put it on.

"Where are we going?"

"Be quiet," she says.

We walk a little ways down the driveway.

"I want to stay here."

"Emma, shut up. Please."

I don't know if she has ever said please to me in my life. I stop moving and drop my grocery bag on the ground. "You're doing this because you think now that I have a period Daddy will want me in the bed and you will have to sleep on the couch," I say.

She grabs my arm and jerks me again. "Are you stupid?"

Before I can answer the back door of the trailer opens and Mama is standing there looking like she would not know which of Mrs. Weston's smiley faces to point to.

"No," she says like she is begging. "Not tonight."

Abigail pushes me behind her and says to Mama, "You stay, then. We're going."

"I'm not going," I say.

"Shut the fuck up," Abigail says.

I try to walk toward Mama but Abigail grabs the hood of my coat and pulls me backward onto the ground and the wind goes out of me in a rush. Mama runs down the stairs like she wants to help me but Abigail gets in her way.

They look at one another for a long time then Abigail starts to cry and Mama starts to cry and I am on the ground still shaking bad from the cold. Mama snatches Abigail to her chest like she has never hugged anyone in her life and when I stand up Abigail grabs me against them with one arm. They are crying like someone has died. The porch light comes on and all of us jerk closer to one another.

When the back door opens Daddy is standing there in his boxers with his Beretta in his hand and we are standing in the orange circle that the porch light makes on the ground. Once he sees we are not criminals he looks closer and sees something much worse.

He doesn't say anything or move. He just stands in the doorway staring at my Mama with the gun against his leg. She and Abigail are looking at him like he is the Devil come to earth and I can't help it but let go and pee runs down my leg.

"You girls go inside," he says, sweet as you please. "It's too cold to be out here."

Mama squeezes us. "Go inside."

Abigail starts walking but my feet are stuck like glue. I cannot stop staring at where he is standing up above us on the porch with the big orange light behind him like a giant shadow. He exhales like he is getting impatient so Abigail turns around and picks me up under my armpits and I wrap my arms and legs around her even though I am too big to be toted.

She takes me right into the bathroom and puts me in the tub

and closes the door. I still can't move or talk and my body is shaking like I am poor Fortunato trapped in the wall. Abigail turns on the water in the sink and in the tub hard as it will go. She kneels down in front of me and covers my ears with her hands and when we are this close together I see we have the same color eyes.

I am supposed to ask my Sunday school class for prayers because my Mama is in the hospital from a terrible car crash and might not live. Daddy stands up during the service and asks the congregation to bow their heads and pray for her too. Abigail didn't say a word to him or me all last night so he put her on the couch and I got to sleep in the bed. He put one hand under my shirt and touched my chest and stomach hard. His body shook for a long time and when he hollered it sounded like he was mad at everything in the world.

Abigail doesn't bow her head when we pray for our Mama to overcome her injuries. Pastor Ryan says that trials happen because of the sin in our hearts and Daddy whispers, "Yes Lord."

Any person or family that wishes to renounce their sin and give themselves to God may come up to the altar and do so during the final hymn but no one ever does. The organist starts playing but Abigail and I never sing so Daddy is the only one singing "His Eye is on the Sparrow." He closes his eyes like the Spirit is in him and Mama always said that it didn't matter how loud or bad a person sings as long as they are singing with a Spirit.

We get to the second verse and I look up and Abigail is crying so hard that her whole body is shaking. Daddy reaches over but she runs down the aisle and falls down a few feet in front of the altar in front of everyone with a thunk that I feel through my shoes. Pastor Ryan puts down his hymnal and puts his hand on her head like he wants to pray for her but she slaps his arm, then sits up on her knees and looks at the cross and I can tell that she is not giving herself to God or anyone else. Daddy stares at her confused and angry that she is make a spectacle of herself and Mama isn't here to handle it.

After a minute Abigail looks over her shoulder at me. Plenty of people have looked at me like they are sad before but no one has ever looked at me this way. Her eyes are in love and scared. We do not belong to God anymore and we can never belong to God again if we ever did to begin with. I walk down the aisle and the closer I get the harder she cries. She grabs me down onto her lap and rocks me back and forth while she cries and before I know it I am crying too just because seeing her cry is insufferable.

Pastor Ryan reaches out again but Abigail gives him a look so ugly that he jerks his hand back like she burned him. She puts her face into my hair and keeps rocking me like she is trying to get me to go to sleep. She stares at the cross like if she could beg hard enough with her eyes God might reach down and pick us both up and carry us in his giant hand out of the church and into heaven itself. But the song ends and the only giant hands we feel are the ones wrapping around our waists to pull us away from the altar.

That night he rolls me belly-up onto his chest and touches me while I stare at the ceiling fan going around. He is so busy with his hands on my stomach and legs that he doesn't hear Abigail leave. I hear her leave because she steps on all the wrong floorboards.

"It's better when you make noise," he says but I lay like a dead person on top of him until I am sure my sister is good and gone. He digs between my legs with his fingers and growls like a bear and I hate him so much that my body wants to go off like a bomb and kill him. When he finally rolls me off of him I lay awake for a long time.

He doesn't even realize she's not there when he wakes up and goes out to the shed. It does not occur to him that it's just him and me now. He will not take me to the hospital to see my Mama even though I have asked him three times and each time he has said, "Why? We don't need her fat ass around here, do we?"

"No, we don't need her fat ass around here."

I am sitting in my armchair with "The Cask of Amontillado" on my lap trying to do my homework before the bus comes to pick me up but I think about Loretta and throw up my cereal. My whole body is shaking like there is something to be afraid of but I'm not sure what that is anymore. Maybe I will just be scared of every little thing for the rest of my life, like I am made from fear and I am made of fear and I'll never remember what it feels like to not be scared.

I'm thinking about a life like that when the gravel in the driveway crunches. I look out of the kitchen window and it is a police car. There is a piece of cereal stuck up in my nose from when I threw up.

Officer Overton is playing on the laptop in his car. When he sees me coming down the porch stairs he steps out and closes the door. He is big and handsome and looks like any good cop on TV. His hair is neat and his shoes are shiny and there is not a single wrinkle in his entire uniform that I can see even though I am sure he is the kind of man who beats up lots of bad guys and walks away from explosions without even turning around to look at them. Dale's wife must be a good wife to keep him looking so good.

"Emma?"

"Yes sir."

He walks with all the gizmos on his big belt squeaking. "I was really sorry to hear about your Mama."

"We are praying that she gets better."

"From her car accident?" he says. He is looking at me the way my counselor does.

"Yes sir."

"I got a letter that I think is from your sister. She okay?"

"She's much better now," I say. The cereal in my nose finally falls back into my throat and I snort and swallow it. He pulls Abigail's letter out of his pocket and plays with it but I can't see what it says. His gun has a big, thick grip on it. "Is that a Glock?" I ask him.

He looks down at his waist. "Oh. Yeah."

"I like it."

"Thank you. Where's your Daddy?"

"In the shed under Bobby Tanner's truck."

He nods and looks over there to make sure I am telling the truth but then he looks back at me and points to my cheek where Abigail hit me with her ring a few days ago. "Did you get hit?"

"No sir." But I did, and I wish Abigail was here to hit me again. My eyes start to leak.

"Hey, hey. That's all right. Can I ask what happened?"

"I got my period." I am scared of him and I don't know what to say. "I'm sorry. I got my period. I'm sorry."

"Happens to the best of us," he says with a little laugh. "That's okay."

"No it's not."

"Where's Abigail, Emma?"

"She's much better now," I say again. "I'm sorry."

Officer Overton kneels down so I am taller than him. "What are you sorry for?"

"Loretta," I say. My insides are going to go up my throat or out my ass one or the other. "And I'm just sorry Abigail wrote you a letter and you had to come down here and deal with us."

"Can you look at me, Emma?"

I can't.

"Emma, can you look at me?"

I can't.

"I'm here because your sister asked for help. If something bad happens you should never be afraid to ask people like me for help. That's why we're here." To me his voice sounds like he is up high and I am falling way down into a hole. "That's why I'm here, right now. So I need for you to not be sorry that I'm here and to never be sorry if I come to see you. It's not your fault that I'm here and I'm here because I want to be."

"Yes sir," I say but I didn't hear one word he said.

"If you're in trouble, there is no where else I'd rather be than right here. Okay?"

"Yes sir."

He smiles and touches me on the top of the head. "Can you get your Daddy for me? I need to talk to him about this letter."

I holler for Daddy. He rolls out from under the truck and wipes his hands. "What do you say, Dale?"

"Hey, Jackson." Officer Overton walks slowly toward the garage. "I'm real sorry about what happened to Sarah. I wish I had been at the wreck to help out. Where was it?"

"Freemont and Thigpen."

"I was on duty and it didn't even come up on my pager."

Daddy stuffs his rag into his pocket. "Didn't call for a fuss. I threw her in my truck and took her in myself."

"You really should call if something like that happens."

"She'll get over it."

"Well, look, I came to talk to you about that," Dale says, resting his hand on the front of his belt. "I went to the hospital this morning to talk to her doctors and get a statement from her."

Daddy stops walking and stares at him for a good long time.

"Emma, can you go in the house for me?" Officer Overton says, all nice.

"She can stay if she wants," Daddy says, mean.

I run inside because Loretta needs me to put her out of her suffering. That is something I can do, instead of just waiting all by myself while everything happens around me. Daddy's Beretta is under he and Abigail's bed, empty with a box of bullets next to it. I stuff my pockets to be sure and go out the back door. The trees are all orange and yellow and red around me, and the ground is covered with leaves and it looks like the world is on fire.

Once I am in the woods I pull the clip out of the gun and rack the slide. I don't want to have to shoot Loretta but putting her out of her suffering is the kind thing to do. I got a certificate for kindness from Ms. Atkins because London Cantrell who is named after a city got her hair caught in a fire extinguisher on the wall and I helped pull it out so that is how I know I am a kind person.

My body is as scared as it's ever been but my brain is saying pop it in the head, pop it in the head. When I get there Loretta is lying down in her bed of leaves and whining. My knees shake so bad that I fall down a few feet away from her the same way my sister fell down in church yesterday.

"My Daddy loves me, and Abigail, and my Mama. But he loves you best."

I look at my Daddy's dog, stand up, and make my stance. I aim at her shoulder but my hands are shaking so bad that I'm scared I will miss. I don't want to hurt her or anything else, even though I am sure it's too late to do enough good things to get back on God's good side if shooting a dog is a good thing at all.

I try counting to three, but my finger is frozen on the trigger because killing a dog does not feel like shooting a wooden target. I try counting down from three. Then I try counting from one to ten and ten to one. I try staring right at her and I try closing my eyes. I try aiming at her eyeball and I try aiming at her nose. I try imagining how happy Loretta will be when she wakes up in heaven and she will think about how nice it was for Emma to put her out of her suffering. But it is too hard.

I put the gun into my pants and peel the rope out of the bloody places on her neck. It takes me a minute of working but I get the knot loose and help her up. She runs away from me and away from our house and I don't blame her. It is not long before I can't see her anymore.

The gun gets heavy. Everything is heavy. My body is too heavy so I lean against the tree with the rope still wrapped around it. There are chiggers on my arm now and the wind tickles the leaves in the trees so that there is noise everywhere and I cannot stand the noise and little sparkles of sun come down and I cannot stand the light. My Daddy is hollering way off on the other side of the woods. After a minute there is one blip of Officer Overton's police siren and then an engine revving and pulling out down the road toward town.

Then my Daddy calls my name. He is angry as a hornet at the world and I do not even have Loretta to make him feel better. I imagine what his face must look like because he is realizing right now that Mama, Abigail, and his dog are all gone and I am the only one he has left to feed him and wash his clothes and sleep with him in his bed. His cheeks and forehead are probably bright red and his hands will be harder than hammers on me until the day I die and only then will it all stop.

There is a Blue Jay sitting on a branch a few trees away from me and in the morning sun it is the prettiest blue I've ever seen in my life, prettier than any paint or crayon or marker could ever be. When my Daddy calls my name again that pretty blue bird gets scared and flies up up and away. I watch until it's gone and then I take a deep breath and hold it hard in my chest like I am hugging the air itself. I lift my Daddy's Beretta and take aim but I don't bother hitting my stance because I know I will not miss.

─────────────

KASEY THORNTON *was born in Wendell, N.C., and received her BA in English from Elon University. She attended both the University of North Carolina at Wilmington and North Carolina State University for her MFA and is working hard on a collection of short stories highlighting oft-overlooked social issues in the South. Her work has been featured in Apeiron Review and Colonnades. She currently resides in the Raleigh-Durham area with her partner, author Kevin Kauffmann.*

Gormley

Chris Arp

I am thinking specifically of Bournemouth in 1837, of that last ball of the summer thrown jointly by the Cruxleys and the Danesworth-Loebs. The memory has slowed with time: the waltzers rotate like the gears of a clock, the women's skirts gather the dust and sweep it in arcs across the floor. I was fifteen years old at the time, and watched all this from a table where I sat with my mother and father, my older brother Lawrence, his new wife Tabitha, and finally her obese cousin, Mr. Fitzwilliam Gormley Kay, who drank glass after glass of cold champagne in an effort, he explained, to stave off perspiration.

"I could have a window opened," I told him.

"I'm sorry, Ewan?"

"I said that I could request they open a window."

"On my account? I forbid it."

He was thirty-seven and a bachelor. After losing his position at the Brice and Bristle sugar concern on Saint Kitts, Mr. Gormley Kay had accepted my mother's invitation to recuperate at our summer estate. He arrived in June with a trunk of unwashed clothing, a stack of scientific texts with the pages uncut, and a large wooden display case of pinned beetles that he referred to, without a jot of irony, as his treasures.

"Did it make the tropics difficult?" I asked. "Your perspiration?"

He displayed his empty glass to a passing servant.

"Unfathomably so."

When Mr. Gormley Kay described the West Indies, he spoke of the heat and the meagerness of the cuisine and of a boredom "that swallows you up like the poor and aged Jonah." My father heard this as self-pity, but I understood him better. For I felt the same about Bournemouth, with its sun-blasted beach, its pastel umbrellas, the jangling of its sweet-seller's carts. What a contrast it was, each afternoon, to go to the door of the guest room and listen to the curious, bird-like sounds of Mr. Gormley Kay's private mutterings.

We were joined at our table by Mr. Quentin Stirk, who held his new pipe as if to present it for inspection.

"Sitting out the polonaise, master Ewan?" he asked me.

"So it seems," said I.

"At your age?" He winked at my mother. "We can't have that, can we, Mrs. Keane?"

For most of the year, Mr. Stirk was a schoolteacher who lived in a two-story cottage on Branksome Dene with an aged mother and aunt. But for the two summer months that he was hired to tutor me in maths, he became something else entirely. For it was not our money that he valued so much as the invitation to society events, where he might show off his purple smoking jacket, his silk d'Orsay, the pocket squares purchased at the Soho Bazaar and—this summer's newest addition—a Meerschaum pipe with a white bell of scrimshawed ivory.

"This one can't be bothered to dance," my mother said, meaning me. "He can't be bothered to do anything save what he's a mind to do."

"Now now, Mrs. Keane! He's clay to be molded! He might think otherwise, but that's why we don't ask his opinion."

This was all puffery, for in truth Mr. Stirk was no taskmaster. His practice was to quiz me on my figures for a quarter hour then move on to sundry subjects, opining now on Welsh Non-conformists, now on Faraday's electric dynamo. He would soliloquize at length, gazing out across the expanse of our back garden, sailing along on the headwind of his own interest.

"Well," my mother said now, fanning herself, "it is a close night, at any rate."

Mr. Stirk set his pipe on the table. "That is due to the

temperature of the ocean," he said. "It is best, Mrs. Keane, to think of the air as a gradient between the emptiness of the upper heavens and the liquid density of—"

"We will see you tomorrow then," my mother said.

She had no patience for a Stirkian discourse. Within the family, the tutor was a figure of fun, part of the Bournemouth flora. Back in London, it was not uncommon to hear her demand that my father "stop being such a Stirk." So now we all looked at the man with the blank faces of concealed mirth. All of us, that is, except for one. For I noticed that Mr. Gormley Kay regarded Mr. Stirk with an interest, even fascination, that his drunkenness laid bare.

Mr. Stirk, accustomed to our sudden chilliness, bowed and took his leave, forgetting altogether his new prize, the fat-bottomed pipe. My father took it up, rotated it to examine the carving and set it down in front of my cousin-in-law.

"An object," he said.

But it was not until later, while my father asked a liveryman to have our carriage harnessed and brought round, that I saw my cousin-in-law slide his hand toward the pipe and touch the mouthpiece where it was still damp.

Such a thing was without precedent in my experience. How can I describe it? There was not, at that first moment, any thought of sensuality, no thrill of the perverse. I might call it an illumination, but in fact it was the opposite—a moment of utmost privacy, a shadow into which no light could enter. I felt a wave of tenderness for Mr. Gormley Kay, toward his transparent desire. I thought it was peculiar and rare. I can still recall it with clarity, when so much else—that whole forsaken era—has faded away.

I requested that Mr. Stirk come to our estate half an hour before our lesson, so that he might join us for lunch. Then I knocked on Mr. Gormley Kay's door to ensure his presence.

Once the tutor arrived, however, my mother did her best to ruin things. For my cousin-in-law, she could not provide enough, offering him the platter of pastries before he had finished his eggs and demanding that Beatrice mix him a sherry cobbler. For Mr. Stirk, however, she gestured toward the stove top, where he was to provide for himself.

"Mr. Stirk," I said when we were seated. "Have you any interest in beetles?"

"In what?"

"In beetles. Cousin Fitzwilliam is a collector."

Mr. Stirk took in, as if for the first time, the rotund man sitting across from him.

"Of *beetles?*"

Mr. Gormley Kay bowed his head. "An amateur. Not even an amateur. Only . . . an appreciator."

"Mr. Gormley Kay is a gentleman scientist," my mother said. "He has travelled widely."

Mr. Stirk's mustache pulsed as he chewed. "Have you been to Minorca, Mr. Gormley Kay?"

"I have not."

"I sailed there once, on vacation with mum. Grand. Burned my thighs to cinders, but very grand." He nodded at my mother. "Bring zinc oxide and a hat, is my point. And a book for the boredom. Though of course the beauty of Spain is a stimulant in itself."

My mother pursed her lips. "I can't imagine that Spain should have anything to offer one such as Fitzwilliam, who has been to the Canary Islands."

"It does sound quite lovely," said Mr. Gormley Kay. He set down his fork. "Minorca, Minorca, Minorca. It is now set in my memory."

After a moment of silence, Mr. Stirk said the word "Travel." Then, a bit later: "It is akin to reading, is it not? A confrontation with the unknown?"

"Precisely so," murmured Mr. Gormley Kay to the napkin spread across his thigh. "What a fine way of phrasing it."

"And," added Mr. Stirk, "one must suppose that Spain has beetles as well."

But here my mother interjected.

"Really, Mr. Stirk. Are you not aware that you are talking to a *specialist?*" She looked at me in sincere horror. "Is it now the fashion to speak of whatever one desires? To say anything, *anything*, so long as it is speech?"

Little was said after this. Mr. Stirk, chastened, could only run a finger along his fork. Mr. Gormley Kay, discomfited at the best of times, gave his muffled thanks and fled to the safety of the guest room. I believed that all was lost.

But two days later, during an afternoon lesson on parabolic equations, who should emerge on the veranda but Mr. Gormley Kay, washed and shaved and dressed in an exquisite and hitherto unseen shirt the color of a bluebonnet. He took a seat not far from us and looked up to observe the clouds.

Mr. Stirk, newly energized by the presence of a guest, placed his finger in the path of my quill. "And what is the inverse of such a function?" he asked.

On a new line, I started the equation anew.

"Tut!" He said. "Not the equation. Alter the *line*."

I looked to Mr. Gormley Kay, then back at Mr. Stirk. "But I cannot, sir. First I must alter the equation, only then can I plot the line."

At which point the young teacher leaned back in his chair, and spoke so that all assembled might hear. "When Menaechmus lectured at the agora of Thrace, Master Ewan, attracting such crowds that it became a matter of civil concern, he did so not with *equations*, but with two bits of string. One green, one red. He had no writing implement, no papyrus. He had no need. He could *see* it, you understand. This distinction you draw between the equation and its representation is illusory."

Here he stood, brushing the crumbs of his digestive biscuits from his lap. "And have they taught you, at that fine school of yours, what led Menaechmus to the discovery of the parabola and the ellipse?"

"They have not, sir."

Mr. Stirk moved to the edge of the paved terrace, so that he spoke against a backdrop of lightly wooded hills, now cast in faint oranges and purples by the descending sun. "The citizens of Delos," Mr. Stirk began, "were racked by internecine strife. Their discord angered Apollo, who sent forth a plague of such destructive power that the Delians were left no corner but to appeal to the oracle at Delphi. Pythia, the high priestess, considered the matter for thirteen days and thirteen nights. Finally, she called upon the Delians and asked them a simple question.

What was the size and shape of their temple of Apollo?"

This was, of course, another Stirkian discourse. But Mr. Gormley Kay's expression bade me listen more attentively.

"Why, the temple is a cube, the Delians replied. The priestess nodded. Double that cube, said she, and assuage Apollo, god of knowledge and the arts. Thus was gifted to posterity the Delian problem. Namely, how to double the volume of a cube, using not weights and winches but pure geometry alone. Menaechmus of Thrace dedicated his *life* to that mystery. Can you fathom such a thing, Master Ewan? His entire life. And herein lies the beauty. That though Menaechmus died a failure in his own eyes, he gave to us his cast-offs—the ellipse, the hyperbola, the parabola—without which the modern world would not exist."

"Wondrous," Mr. Gormley Kay murmured from his chair. "And wondrous sad."

Mr. Stirk nodded. Behind him the sun had nearly set. Fireflies like winking stars glimmered across the lawn. How different the tutor appeared in such a light. His thin frame, all slopes and curves, appeared more singular, more poised. It was the first time in my life that a man shrugged off the ridiculousness and comedy in which I had clothed him.

"And that is not the most wondrous part," Mr. Stirk concluded. "It took a mind such as Plato's to understand the oracle's true meaning. For the *Delian problem*, Plato explains, demonstrates that the mathematical imagination alone can o'erthrow the passions that had doomed the citizens of Delos. When you can *picture* the parabolic function, Master Ewan, in the mind's eye, then inverting that function is akin to turning a pirouette. It is an act of … of …"

Here he paused, searching for the word.

"Cessation," Mr. Gormley Kay offered.

This was not what Mr. Stirk had in mind. But he blessed it regardless with a mild little nod.

Many will insist that I was motivated by prurient curiosity, that their physical union—a kernel of joy surrounded by such pungent shame—stirred my imagination. Perhaps. But if this is true, it is only a component of a larger truth. What I found so captivating in their relationship was that it was unmentionable. I thought of Mr. Stirk and Mr. Gormley Kay as evening primroses or catchflies, those flowers that open only in the quiet of night, drawing their strength from the darkness, from the moon, from the moths that glide on the cold winds off the ocean.

The beetles appeared more fragile than I'd anticipated, more like ornate replicas fashioned from wire, tissue and glue. Many of them glistened like spilled oil. Mr. Gormley Kay, without a trace of his customary anxiety, tapped the glass above a small fellow spotted with green and gold.

"*Omophroninae carabidae*," he said. "Native to Hispaniola."

This was two days later. After observing another lesson, Mr. Gormley Kay had invited the two of us to his room, where the bed was unmade and great heaps of clothing filled the chairs. The smell was intimate and sharp.

"You've been to Hispaniola, then?" Mr. Stirk asked.

"No, no. For most of these I sent away. There's a sort of organization, you could call it. We exchange research, samples. Money is at times involved, but only when necessary, and never enough to sully the water."

"A type of society, then? An explorer's society?"

"If you like."

Mr. Stirk turned to me. "I rather think I would like it. Every week a letter from Siam? From Katmandu?" He leaned over the beetles. "I wonder what I'd write back. Who's this fellow?"

"*Allomyrina dichomata*. But the Japanese call him," Mr. Gormley Kay pronounced the word with solemnity: "*kabutomushi*."

"He's a little lord, isn't he?"

"Absolutely correct. It's the proboscis."

"That means nose," Mr. Stirk said to me. Then he whispered to Mr. Gormley Kay. "Expensive?"

"Well. There's a limit, of course. But yes, he's right there at the limit, there's no doubt about that."

Mr. Stirk stepped back to take in the whole arrangement. "My word," he said and clucked his tongue. "My sun and stars, but they are gorgeous. Evidence of the Lord's generosity. Proof not only of his divine presence," he said, "but of his personal touch."

Mr. Gormley Kay nodded. "I entirely agree, Mr. Stirk."

"Quentin, please. Call me Quentin."

"Very well," Mr. Gormley Kay said, tentatively. "Quentin."

"Are you heading out again any time soon?" Mr. Stirk asked. "To the tropics?"

"I've given it a great deal of thought," my cousin-in-law replied. "I am of two minds completely. Part of me is desperate to leave, for I've always hated England and everyone in it. But part of me . . . part of me would very much like to stay."

"Well," said Mr. Stirk. "If you do leave, you should provide me with your address. I've never received a letter from farther afield than Sunderland. I should find it rather a treat."

The following weekend was the last of the summer. We had a tradition of taking a picnic basket out to the New Forest, and I invited Mr. Stirk along.

"It will mean an extra sandwich," my mother said. "And olives. The man behaves as if they were shipped from Greece for his pleasure alone."

He sat next to the driver and acted as our guide, knocking on the roof with his cane whenever we passed sites of local importance: the tree that women kissed when they wanted a baby, the trail along which his aunt gathered hibiscus, a field whose fallowness testified to the sloth of the family that owned it. Mr. Gormley Kay meanwhile pressed his face against the window, the coolness of which, he explained, was a balm for his nausea.

After lunch, I suggested the men accompany me to our swimming hole, a deep eddy off the Lymington River. After some minutes of paddling about, my father removed himself, and my brother followed soon after. The three of us floated there together, our bodies pink and hazy beneath the water. Mr. Gormley Kay rolled onto his back and floated in a most impressive way, the whole mountain of him rising above the surface, from chest to toe, shining and goose-pimpled by the occasional breeze. Every now and then his penis broke the surface like the mouth of a carp.

"How buoyant he is!" I said to Mr. Stirk.

The tutor attempted it himself but from the neck down remained submerged. "Too dense," he said miserably. "Too dense by far."

"There's no trick to it," said Mr. Gormley Kay. "One has to

have faith that one's head will not go under. Lean back . . . and submit."

For nigh on an hour we floated, the only sounds the gentle movement of the trees, the river's ticklish trickle, the occasional splash and splutter of Mr. Stirk's efforts. Water filled my ears with a little clap, then drained away.

"There," I heard Mr. Gormley Kay murmur. "Now you've got it." And it was true. Mr. Stirk's knees and sharp ribs could be seen above the water, as well as the wet mass of brown hair that gathered like algae in the valley of his chest. His eyes were closed tight, his breathing labored and short.

We returned home later than we had planned. I suggested that Mr. Stirk stay and spare the horses the journey to Branksome Dene. He agreed and joined us that night by the drawing room fire. In all our time at Bournemouth, Mr. Gormley Kay had never participated in these evening conversations, but now he appeared in his loose flannel nightclothes, in such a fine mood that when Beatrice inquired as to his choice of liqueur, he put on a little performance of consideration—a deep frown, a hard squint. "Just a drop—two drops at *most*—of créme de cassis."

He took a new pleasure in our company, rocking back in his chair to emit his short, high giggle. When my mother commented on how cool the nights were becoming, he shook his head and spoke wistfully. "There was a time when I thought I would never be cool again."

Mr. Stirk, who had hardly said a word, now asked a question. "And was it so horrible in Saint Kitts? Were there no moments of romance or adventure?"

Mr. Gormley Kay gave this some thought. "I don't know how familiar you are with sugar work," he said. "First there is the long planting season, followed by a short refining period of terrible intensity. One hour in the boiler-room is enough to leave you entirely hairless. And if you believe that hell smells of brimstone, you are wrong. It stinks of boiling sugar and coal smoke. At the mill, we hire a fellow to stand with a machete held aloft, in case someone's arm should be caught in the thresher.

"It is well known throughout the trade that during this period of excruciating labor, the refiners and especially the clayers cannot resist the appeal of thievery. This is due not," Mr. Gormley Kay raised a finger, "to their race, but to the long hours and constant heat, which combine to wear down a man's moral instinct. And so at the end of each shift we had to . . . we had to search their pockets.

"This was, I assure you, the most odious moment of an odious job. Here you have this poor man, his lot improved not an inch since liberation, tired and underfed, mutilated and scorched. And here am I, pink and shining from the office heat, redolent with the astringent odor white men give off in equatorial places. I can't look him in the eye, nor he in mine. Our souls two foreign things, like distant stars.

"But then one day, I reached into a fellow's pocket and felt a terrible pinch. I swore and removed my hand, there to find dangling from my finger a tiny, blue crab. I shook it off and shrieked again. And what should follow but a veritable eruption of laughter! All the workers were laughing like you've never heard, laughter to make the ground shake. And when I stumbled and landed on my bottom? Such joy that caused. Such spontaneous, human joy, as striking, incongruous and beautiful as Christ among the money-changers. How happy I was to be its cause. So I made a show of it, shaking my finger and sucking on it like a boy.

"I must have been the talk of the black salons, for it wasn't the very next day that the workers greeted me with great smiles and pantomimes of my now famous reaction. And what should I find that evening but crabs in half the pockets I searched. Of course I learned to spot the telltale bulge, but in I went, then a snap and a cry and sometimes even a comic jig to stoke their merriment. How could I do otherwise? After all, these men had endured the snipping and pinching in their trouser pockets throughout their wretched day. If they suffered for this bit of fun, then so would I. This lasted the duration of that refining period. My fingers were quite scissored to bits. Here. I can prove it."

He raised his hands from his lap. The tips of his fingers were dotted with small white spots like flakes of ash. He invited us to come and look, and indeed we did, but only Mr. Stirk was bold enough to take each one and rotate it in the light of the fire to get a better view.

Afterward, Mr. Gormley Kay regarded his hands for a moment. "I suppose," he said, "that I'll be quite disfigured for the rest of my life."

I insisted that Mr. Stirk sleep in my room, which shared a hallway with that of my cousin-in-law. For myself I made a bed of the sofa beneath the drawing room's tapestry of St. George. It was my plan to stay awake, then creep like a mouse to the keyhole at the guest room door. Watching the way Mr. Stirk held Mr. Gormley Kay's fingers, I felt certain, completely certain, that I would see something unprecedented in our Bournemouth home. But before I could execute my plan, I had to wait for my mother and sister-in-law, who remained at the far side of the drawing room. Their whispering carried over the stir and crackle of the fire.

"I don't know if I can ever thank you enough," said Tabitha.

"Nonsense. It's a pleasure."

"Sweet of you to say. When we were children, he was so withdrawn. No facility at all in his studies, nor in anything else. We used to worry so, and tell ourselves, just wait, just wait. Everyone finds their proper place."

"That is the hope."

"And now, I feel such . . . such guilt."

"You feel responsibility for him."

"I do."

"It's because you are charitable. I can give no higher compliment. You have a charitable soul." Then my mother said: "But one must be charitable to oneself as well. And one can only attempt so much."

She was speaking of me, of course. I had heard much the same and worse, but for the first time I was not bothered. Quite the opposite. It was a pleasure to listen to their pity and condescension, knowing what was about to happen—what might already be happening—under the same roof. And perhaps it was this sense of satisfaction that did me in: my mother chattered on; I fell asleep.

When I woke, Stirk was gone and the rest of the family in high agitation. Mr. Gormley Kay, I soon learned, had insisted that he leave that very morning. Our horses were still recovering, so my father had to beg a pair off our neighbors. I asked where Mr. Gormley Kay was.

"Packing his bags," Tabitha said, in tears over the imposition. My mother caressed her hand.

So I sat in the drawing room and watched the hallway. Soon enough, the carriage was announced and the great mass of Mr. Gormley Kay went swiftly by, hauling his luggage two to an arm. He did not see me, nor did I call out to him. His head was nearly purple with strain, his single adieu little more than a squeak.

In time this departure would become the stuff of family legend. The word "gormley" became an adjective meaning faulty, awkward and inexplicable. When Edward "Boy" Jones was caught lurking in the Queen's dressing room and shipped off to Tothill Fields, my father's comment was brief: "Another gormley chap expunged." And when the news of Mr. Gormley Kay's death reached us some six years later, the details all seemed to confirm the word. His body was discovered in Burma, where he worked as a junior administrator in the new government and was locally famous for his advanced dissipation. We heard a few "gormley stories," like when he encouraged the local children to leap on his back and made of himself a sort of drunken omnibus, lurching across the cobblestones and embarrassing the Crown.

But at the time, watching him flee, I felt snubbed. As soon as he was gone, I took a branch to the edge of the lawn and spent an hour whipping the leaves from the young dogwood tree that was my mother's favorite. This done, I went to the guest room. Beatrice had not yet cleaned; the bedclothes lay twisted at the foot of the mattress, clouded glasses lined the window sill. Tucked away in a corner stood the large wooden case, partially obscured by a curtain. For a moment, I believed he had left it for me, but when I set it on the bed it tinkled faintly. I opened it and saw the fractured panes of glass. The insects beneath were crushed to fragments, the white lining soiled by their dust. And there, among the shards of carapace and legs, was a trail of brown, faded blood.

I knew the cause: the two had met in the night and quarreled. Mr. Gormley Kay had confessed his feelings. Mr. Stirk flew into a rage and destroyed what was most dear and close to hand. Then he fled.

I had misjudged. I saw the shattered case as my own responsibility. But it was not guilt I felt at that moment, not precisely. More than anything, I felt young. Or perhaps it is more accurate to say that I felt myself to be the age I was.

I suppose the intervening decades have been the greatest England has ever known. As children, we might have read William Wilberforce and *Am I Not A Man And A Brother?*, but the schoolboys of today have read far more. They can speak as eloquently of Mahommah Baquaqua and Frederick Douglass as they can of labor conditions and the Chartists. I have done my paltry bit in the name of the brotherhood of man. As a young journalist, I attended the World Anti-Slavery Convention, and described Thomas Fowell Buxton addressing the standing crowd. More recently, my pen spread word of the American John Brown and protested those imports the make of Lancashire a stain on the soul of the Empire.

We live in the epoch of societies and lecture halls. There is not an evening without some gathering where we might drink from the fount of heroism and self-sacrifice, usually for less than a farthing. It is my duty to attend as many of these as my editor commands, and it was in this capacity that I came across a notice for the Presbyterian Humane Society and the speech they would be hosting at Saint Bartholomew-the-Less. Much of the poster was given to an illustration of the speaker, a Mr. Quentin Stirk, celebrated abolitionist of Bournemouth.

I registered the face before the name. The expression was not—as is so often the case—ostentatious in its piety or wisdom. In a bit of strategy, the notice presented all the imperfections of advanced old age, the pate bare, the white hairs above the ears uncombed. It was an arresting image; only after a moment did I recognize those eager eyes, the faint droop of the lip beneath a white mustache. I made a note in my daybook.

After that summer, we never hired him on again. There was no need. I lost my place at Harrow, charged quite fairly with "slackness of spirit." He no longer attended society events, and the balls themselves were nearly gone by the fifties, victim to the general withdrawal of the gentry from the public eye.

I did meet him once—this was shortly after Mr. Gormley Kay's death—on Cranborne Road. After bidding him good evening, I glanced at his hands for any sign of a cut or scar. There was none, nor any trace of anger or remorse in his demeanor. Instead there was only the subdued, comradely and ironic expression of a man who has spent all his life in one place.

I understood then that I had it wrong. Mr. Stirk never went to the guest room that night. Instead, Mr. Gormley Kay had himself broken the case, not in the heat of argument but in a moment of obscure and private rage, as a prisoner will strike his head against the bars of his cell—suddenly, and only once.

This realization was important. It served as a warning, clear as a church bell. My interest in gormliness—that curdled solitude, that shadowed place, those incommunicable movements of the soul—it was founded on a mistake. Yes, both Mr. Stirk and Mr. Gormley Kay had blossomed and grown in the time I knew them, but they had grown toward loneliness, toward failure, toward death. It has been said that every contented man charts his course by the suicides of those he once knew. I learned to develop my taste for the more quotidian pleasures—commerce and politics, gossip and drink—the ones that, however dull, lead to family and fine company and laughter.

The audience assembled at Saint Bartholomew-the-Less was elderly and ill-at-ease. These were members of the shop-owning class, with none of the University boys nor East End collectivists that one might expect from the papers. No, this would be a lecture of a type that is rarely reported: an apologia for abolitionism, designed for those too aged or obstinate to see the appeal in the liberal cause. Such lectures happen all the time in London, and provide something of a circuit for the lesser oratorical lights. When Quentin Stirk presented himself, it was to an audience of men gazing up at the eaves and women leafing through their books of common prayer.

"I come tonight," he began, "to speak of simplicity. The simplicity of virtue . . . and the simplicity of sin."

He looked much healthier than the man on the poster. Certainly he was old, but with a straight back and a fine, durable voice.

"We all know the story of Achan, son of Karmi, son of Zimri, son of Zerah. We know from the book of Joshua that during the sack of Jericho this Achan defied God's orders and took for himself a beautiful Babylonian robe, two hundred silver shekels and two hundred of gold. We know that once confronted, this Achan readily confessed his crime and lead his accusers to the hiding place. We know, finally, that the lord high God's judgment was that the Israelites should stone this Achan and burn him. All this we know. And we know furthermore that it was not just Achan who was burned, but the Babylonian robe as well, and the shekels, with which the Israelites might have eased their burden. And not just the robe and the shekels but Achan's wife was burned, and his sons and daughters were burned. And his cattle. And his donkeys. And his sheep."

Cunning to open with a biblical obscurity. Quite a few in the audience, self-conscious before their neighbors, nodded to prove their familiarity with the tale.

"But what we do *not* know," he continued, "is the answer to the most important question of all. Why burn the sheep? Burn Achan, of course. He committed the crime. The robe and shekels? Absolutely, they were the ill-gotten goods. The wife, fine. She would have worn the robe. The children? Oh yes. For they would have profited from the shekels. The *cattle*? Yes, my friends, even the cattle! For as those of us who work with them know, cows are not as simple as they seem. They know of man's work, man's needs. They are, in this sense, complicit. The donkey is harder to accuse, but not impossible. For though the donkey knows not the reason for his servility, still he serves regardless. His lack of discrimination is his undoing. But what of the sheep? If the sheep is known for anything, it is innocence. After all, 'He tends his flock like a shepherd; he gathers the lambs in his arms and carries them close to his heart.' When God commanded that the Israelites burn even the sheep, did he speak in error?"

By which point he had his audience. Glancing about, I saw faces slack with attention, all eyes fast on the man before them. Mr. Stirk had learned that a soft voice commanded more attention than a loud one, that a leisurely pace was more entrancing than a trot. He spoke with the naturalness and intimacy of one who had enjoyed attention all his life. There was no denying it. Mr. Stirk had greatly improved.

"How great a gap exists between Achan and the lamb?" he asked his audience. "Morally speaking, how many leagues lie between the one and the other? One might ask a similar question. How great a gap exists between yourself and the Louisiana slaver? An ocean, at the very least. You have never met this man, never supped with him or prayed with him. You have abstained from buying his rice. You know not his name nor face, you hardly understand him when he speaks."

Watching him, I recalled that evening on the verandah, when the young teacher transformed before our eyes. This old man at the pulpit had captured that glimmer of dignity and cultivated it over the years, shaping and molding it, buffing it to a high polish so that now he could display his gifts before any audience, in any venue.

I do not mean that he was performative. I mean that his splendidness no longer belonged to me and Mr. Gormley Kay. It no longer belonged to the past. What I felt, watching him, was that I had lost something precious. I felt, queer as it may sound, as if I had lost a piece of myself. This was the pettiest sort of jealousy, unbecoming in the young and unthinkable in a man of my years. I strained to push this away. I strained to be more magnanimous, more mature.

"Hearken unto God," Mr. Stirk said. "Hearken unto the lamb of Achan. For it is with the lamb's blood that God teaches us the nature of sin, which spreads like fat across the pan. Sin is not the product of activity, dear friends, but of inactivity. Sin does not arise from what we do, but from what we do not. Even the lamb will be killed, brothers and sisters. Even the lamb."

―――――――

CHRIS ARP'S *stories have appeared in Memorious, Storgy Magazine and the Cumberland River Review. He is a graduate of NYU's Creative Writing Program, where he was a finalist for the Axinn Foundation / E.L. Doctorow Fellowship. His stories have been selected as finalists for the Rick DeMarinis Short Story Contest and the Cincinnati Review Award, and another was recently nominated for a Pushcart Prize. He is currently working on a novel.*

www.chrisarp.com

Confessions of a Lady-In-Waiting

Rachel Engelman

I was in love with the Queen. We all were, in a way. As lady's maids, it was a risk of the job. Our sole task on earth was to adore her, entertain her, make the hours of her life fly by. We oiled her feet, combed her hair, rubbed the little knots out of her back. We laced her into dresses, wrapped pearls around her neck, braided gold wire into her hair. We undressed her at the end of the day and tucked her in at night, though she was old enough to be most of our mothers.

There were other things that we could not speak of. We got rid of babies—the ones that came too early, their faces like wet clay. We wrapped them in cloth and buried them in the rose garden. The King could never know. It would have been bad for business. In those days, it was only too easy for a King to get rid of a Queen.

What else? We made her break off affairs when they went too far. The Queen was a passionate woman, and passion made her reckless. We always knew when it was time. We would tell her: *Let him go, now, before someone gets killed.* It made us a little sick with ourselves, sending away the man who had made our lady glow.

There were other, less glamorous chores. We plucked ingrown

hairs, burned off warts, scraped heels and elbows to leave the skin as soft as soap. We painted her nipples a comely pink for parties. Soaked her underwear in rose water, clipped the fine curls between her legs.

The Queen was Spanish, with high, white cheekbones and eyes like split olives. Her hair was a mess of dark coils. She had a rubbery mole above her upper lip. Her body was frail, her breasts unfashionably small. Sometimes for special occasions, we plumped them up with little pillows.

The King, predictably, went for women with big swaying tits, and asses as fat as donkeys'. To be a lady-in-waiting was to be in constant risk of the King's affections. Even the youngest and greediest among us could not muster up an appetite for the King. He was a fat, hateful man with a beard in which one could always find bits of fried egg. His teeth were yellow and long, his eyes bloodshot, his breath like rotten chicken.

If he desired one of us, he would send a note. The girl would be bathed, oiled, and repaired to a dark room at the top of the north tower. There, the King would subject her to his violent love. The unlucky girl always came back with bruises and welts, once, a missing tooth.

We comforted her. We held her in our arms. We told her it was good to cry.

If a lady's maid became pregnant by the King, she was sent to the country to await the child. Boys were kept, girls were gotten rid of. The boys became little court demons—brats with loose titles and no respect for anything. They terrorized kitchen maids, beat stable boys, cut the tails off cats, and slaughtered the King's wild boars for sport. Their job was to grow up and wait. If the Queen did not produce a male heir, the worthiest among them would be crowned.

For this was the sad truth: the Queen could not bear sons. The only thing that ever came out of her were daughters. She had had five by the time I came to the castle.

The daughters lived in a manor at the very edge of the King's lands. The Queen was forbidden to visit, for the King thought it improper—she should be concentrating on bearing sons, not gallivanting with a bunch of stupid girls. Her job was to lie prone all day, dreaming of little penises.

Every lady's maid had a special talent. Joselyn was a genius with the removal of hair; Yvonne had a gift for makeup and lancing boils. Ursuline was skillful at the harp, and Tamor brewed an herbal tea that made us hallucinate.

I wasn't good at anything, except hunting. With my bow and arrow, I could hit a moth in a crowd of butterflies. This was not considered a great skill among the lady's maids, but the Queen found it novel.

I remember the day I taught her to shoot. She kicked her little heels when her arrows flew awry. But just as the sky turned gold, she shot a dove clean through the head. I remember her face, sweaty and exultant, her smile showing a row of small, pointed teeth.

I learned my skill in the forests of Italy, where I was born. I had never wanted to be a lady's maid. As a child, I heard tales of the French castles—how the women were forced into dresses that twisted their organs, and shoes so small they had to slice off offending toes. I did not dream of a courtly life—I'd been perfectly content hunting rabbits, teaching my young brothers to dance, sleeping under the trees.

But I was young, handsome, and unmarried. Several men had asked for my hand, but I'd scared them off. I told them that I'd fornicated with the devil, and that any penis that entered my body would shrivel up like a dried snake.

God-fearing men are so easy to fool!

Still. One of the King's emissaries saw me hunting in the forest and captured me. He thought the Queen would like the idea of an exotic lady's maid. So he bound me, gagged me, and took me back to France.

I remember my first day at the castle. I was shut up alone in the Queen's chamber—a great vaulted room with ochre walls and round crystal windows. Animal skins lay across the floor in descending order of size—bear, wolf, fox. The bed was a monstrous contraption with curved sideboards like a sleigh, accessed by a set of golden stairs.

The other lady's maids filed into the room and circled around me. They pinched my hips and pointed at my thick eyebrows. Called me, *le petite gorille*.

When the Queen appeared, they fell silent.

I stared at her. She was smaller than me by a head, but instantly I felt like a child before her, stupid and blundering. The Queen walked around me in a circle, then stopped to touch my chin.

Such luscious eyebrows, she said.

The other girls snorted.

Taisez-vous! she hissed.

Your eyes are angry, *ma chérie,* she said. Like bees stuck in a jar.

No, I lied. I'm glad to be here.

She laughed—a high tinkling sound like breaking glass.

You're a bad liar. Just like the rest of these idiots, she said, waving at the other lady's maids. What is your name?

I told her, and she said, No, that won't do. She touched my cheek. I will call you *ma poule*, for you will be my little chicken—the pet of my heart.

My first weeks at the castle were lonely. I was not accustomed to sleeping in a bed at night, let alone in a room with four other lady's maids. Ours was a bleak chamber, with frozen stone floors and walls that pearled with dark water. The windows were inlaid with ruby glass, so the light that poured into the room was bloody. We slept in narrow beds closed off by curtains, behind which the other girls would weep, fart, and pleasure themselves. I spent my nights staring up at the ceiling, dreaming of the Umbrian sky.

My very first morning, my shift was stripped from my body and thrown into the fire. Ursuline and Joselyn bathed me, scrubbed me, and stuffed me into a corset. The whalebones shoved my breasts up to the base of my neck and crowded my organs. My face was powdered, my cheeks painted with red blobs, and my hair tied back so tightly that it pulled my eyes into slits.

Before I could complain, Ursuline sprayed me with perfume.

You smell like a chicken yard, she said. *Mon dieu!*

The King banned the use of "heathen tongues," which included my Italian and the Queen's own Spanish. I tried to harness my accent, but the girls still snorted whenever I spoke.

Shoes were another burden. I was used to going barefoot, or

in leather slippers. Now I was made to clatter around in slippers with sharp wooden heels. My toes were forever catching on rough stones, pitching me onto my knees.

The other lady's maids found this hilarious. They found most things I did hilarious. I would smile at their laughter and whisper, *rotting whore*, or *shit eater*, in Turkish.

Yet, after a time, we became reluctant friends. We were the sole witnesses to each other's heartbreaks—the deaths of mothers far away, the losses of lovers. And then there were the bodily illnesses that we passed onto each other like fleas—fevers and poxes and rashes. Even I, wild girl that I was, could not deny sisterhood after a night of shitting and vomiting into the same bowl.

Gradually, over time, they schooled me in the Queen's likes and dislikes. She hated to be woken in the midst of a nightmare. She loathed shellfish and was scared of crows. There were certain topics that were forbidden: the Spanish court, her daughters, men named Rosenthal or Montague.

And what of her pleasures?

She loved to dance, to smoke her long golden pipe, to get drunk off wine. To nibble on truffles, to imitate clergymen. When she drank, she cursed in Spanish, and if she was very far gone, she sang lullabies with a sibilant "*s*."

When I arrived at the castle, the Queen had just come to the end of her longest affair. The lover—a Portuguese knight twenty years her junior—had been sent back to his country to marry a cousin. The Queen wept for a week. She refused to eat or wash her hair.

Ma poule, she said to me. I can hear my heart breaking. It sounds like someone stepping on a twig.

A few days later, she called me to her bed.

Get my cloak, she said. I want to pick wildflowers.

She led me past the gates to a shed I had never seen before. Outside stood an old brown mare harnessed to a cherry wood carriage.

You can drive, can't you? she asked.

Yes, but what for? I said. There are flowers all around us.

Oh, I don't want *these*, said the Queen, kicking at a bloom with her toe. I want the ones that grow far off.

We drove for hours. I asked her again and again if we should not turn back, but she only waved her hand. The landscape changed—the tame gardens of the kingdom gave way to the open countryside, covered in horse chestnuts and spiky hawthorns. The brush was full of grouse, and my fingers itched for my bow.

Finally, the Queen told me to stop at the foot of a hill. We left the carriage and walked up a long straight driveway framed by beach trees, at the end of which stood a stone manor covered in vines. A row of chimneys stuck out from the roof like a crown. Wild flowers grew all around, and chalky butterflies dipped in and out of pools of light.

What is this place? I asked.

She gave me a quick smile, then pulled me behind a tree. From a sack she produced two plain shifts—peasant's dresses, coarse and brown. Then a black ribbon, which she tied around her face, covering her eyes.

We are women from the neighboring village, she said. I am blind, and you are my keeper. We've come to beg water and bread for our journey home.

Before I could argue, she walked up to the front door and knocked.

An old woman in a pleated gray dress opened the door. At the sight of the Queen, her face split into a smile.

Oui, Madam? she said loudly.

We crave water and bread. And to sit for a spell.

But of course! The woman cried, taking the Queen's arm. The little mademoiselles are in the garden. Please come.

She led us to a yard lined with flowering cherry trees. On the grass lay a blanket, upon which sat five small girls. The oldest could have been no older than ten. The youngest was a baby lying on her stomach. They all wore pale pink dresses. They each had coiled black hair.

Children! cried the woman in gray. Do you remember my friend, the lady from the village? Come greet her.

The girls—all except the baby—left their blanket and gathered around us.

Bonjour, they said, touching their skirts.

But for shame! teased the Queen. The King's own children do not speak *Anglais*?

We *do*, said a small girl with fat cheeks. Why, we can even *sing*!

Ah, but you must be very clever! said the Queen.

Oh, *oui Madam*, said the girl, sticking a finger in her nose.

I remember *you*, said the oldest—a pale creature with a mole above her lip. She sniffed the Queen's hand. You smell like flowers.

For an hour, I sat in the shade of a tree and watched as the girls hopped around the Queen, chattering and singing. They recited poems and performed clumsy waltzes. The oldest girl imitated a string of forest birds. A pudgy child with giant eyes did an impression of a fainting goat. The baby was placed in the Queen's lap and fell asleep against her breast.

As the sun began to fade, the Queen rose abruptly, handing the baby back to the old woman. She produced a small bag of white chocolates, carved into rose buds.

But Madam, it is too much! said the woman.

No, said the Queen darkly. It will never be enough.

She rose and took my arm. We left the house to the sound of the girls crying, *Au revoir! Come back soon!*

Outside the gate, the Queen pulled the ribbon from her face. Her eyes were damp. We walked toward the carriage.

It's my only way to see them, she said at last. I do it once a year. She stopped walking and stared at her feet. There is no hell like being ripped from your daughters. Most mornings I dream of a window I can jump out of.

You mustn't talk like that, I said, pulling the shift over my head.

Why not?

Because it frightens me.

If I did, you'd have a new Queen—one that could produce male heirs.

Stop it! I said, heat flashing in my cheeks.

She looked at me, amused.

If you died, I would have to die too, I said.

What foolishness is this? she said.

It's my job. I am never to leave you alone.

So you're a dog, now?

I looked at her. Into her black eyes. Into her mocking smile.

Yes, I said. I'm a dog.

We changed dresses and climbed into the carriage. The sun had set and the sky turned a dusty indigo. The night owls hooted as we rode back in silence. When we arrived at the castle, we tied the horses up beside the shed. The Queen touched my arm.

You are not a dog, she said softly. You are *ma poule*.

Often, the other lady's maids would be sent off on far-flung errands—to procure creams or rare silks or to deliver messages. I was left alone with the Queen. While I polished her rings, or sewed pearls onto her gowns, we would talk. She told me about her girlhood in Spain, her lovers, her fondness for marbled ham.

Have you ever been in love? she asked.

No, I said. A few men desired me, but I got rid of them. I told her, cautiously, of my trick with the devil. She stared at me, then burst into laughter.

Oh, *ma chérie*! she said. You are even crazier than I thought.

The other ladies-in-waiting were constantly having affairs. The noblemen charmed them with petty gifts—whicker dolls, clay bracelets, bunches of grapes. The knights got them drunk in the woods and let them play with their swords. The less choosy girls lay with stable boys—they were supposed to be the most tender—so gentle with horses.

You should keep your eyes peeled, said Tamor. Or you'll end up alone.

But the men in court made me sick. The way they sucked marrow from bones and guzzled their wine. I hated their oiled mustaches and pale little hands.

At court, it was all bowing and hand-kissing. How are you finding our beloved country? They asked. And, *What a charming accent you have!*

Yet, these were the same men that raped kitchen maids in the middle of the night. I could hear their screams from my bedroom window.

Whenever I could, I spat in their wine. I called them *rotting dick* and *dog piles* in Turkish.

Charming! they exclaimed. What's that mean?

Alabaster angel, I said.

One day, a band of Spaniards came to the castle—a master sword-maker and his three sons. The youngest, a boy with a pointed beard and bright red lips, grinned at me during the feast. I watched as he plunged his hand into a pheasant and brought out the giblets, glistening like jewels.

Afterward, he cornered me in a hallway.

You are *muy bella*, he said. Just like my horse.

Get away from me, I spat, shoving past him.

He pushed me against a wall and gave my nipple a brutal twist.

I can tell you like me, *bella*, he said.

Come near me ever again, I said. And I'll cut your dick off.

But two days later, on my way back from gathering hazelnuts, I had no knife. He dragged me behind the stables and threw me onto a pile of manure. There, he tore off my stockings. I tried to scream, but he gagged me with his cape.

The only mercy was that it was quick. A few frenzied strokes, and he was panting on top of me, limp as a corpse. I shoved him off and he rolled down the pile of manure.

Tell anyone, *bella*, he said. And your name will be ruined. No man will ever marry you.

I ran back to my chamber and tore off my dress. I touched myself between the legs and began to scream.

Joselyn came in and pinched her nose. What in God's name do you smell like? she cried.

I lifted my skirt and showed her the welts on the inside of my thighs.

She closed her eyes. *Monstre*, she whispered. She came and wrapped her arms around me. Come, sister, she said. Let me clean you.

Later that evening, the Queen ordered me to her chamber. When I entered, she was sitting on the bed in her golden dressing gown.

Come, my poor *poule*, she said, and patted the place next to her.

I sat down, but refused to look at her.

Do not be ashamed, she said, touching my cheek. Did no one tell you that men are swine? That all they want is a fresh cunt? It's a miracle you lasted this long. Why, I was ravaged by own uncle when I was ten.

How can they do it? I asked.

Very easily, I'm afraid, she said.

Not *them*! I snorted. Ursuline and Joselyn and the rest? How can they go to them *willingly*?

Oh, *mon chérie*, it's quite different. It can be beautiful when you're in love. She leaned forward and kissed my forehead. The ghost of a kiss, soft as a shadow. Then she lay me down and wrapped her arms around me.

Sleep now, she said. Not another thought. Not another word.

And because it was an order from the Queen, I shut my eyes.

I always thought that I would feel the loss of my virginity—that it would be like losing a fingernail or a tooth. But in a few weeks, after the bruises healed, and I was sure I would not bear a bastard, I hardly ever thought of it. The only difference was that I no longer dreamed about Italy. It was easier to pretend that I had been born in my bloody chamber, with dry eyes and a cold heart, my chest tied up with strings.

Around this time, the Queen began to have trouble sleeping. When we came to dress her in the morning, the skin beneath her eyes would be wrinkled as walnuts. She slept better when one of us watched over her. The lady-in-waiting would pluck at a lute or read from a book. It was I who was summoned most often. I would stare at her for long hours as she turned her head and made little groans. Often, even after her breathing steadied, I would stay on, creeping away only when the light was coming in through the windows.

One night as I sat in my chair, she turned to me.

Come, *ma poule*. I crave a body next to me.

I climbed the golden stairs and lay down beside her. I could feel the thick embroidery of birds and peaches through my shift. The Queen wrapped her arms around me as she had so many weeks ago, and we slept.

When I awoke in the middle of the night, I turned to find her gazing at me with her big black eyes.

You whisper in your sleep, she said. And you snore like a little pig.

I'm sorry, I said.

She laughed, and smoothed my eyebrows with her fingers. She kissed my cheek, then my chin, then the corner of my mouth. One hand traveled down my neck and came to rest on my breasts.

I want to show you how it can be, she said. I told, you, it's different when you're in love.

But who loves me? I said.

She laughed out loud.

Oh, *ma poule*! Don't be such a child for once.

After that, I was hers. We were discreet during the day—or as discreet as the Queen could be. We did not kiss in front of the other lady's maids—nor did we grope in the passageways. But when we found ourselves alone in her chamber, or met in an empty hall, the Queen would laugh and press me against the wall. Whisper all the things she would do to me later.

Each night, I rapped softly on her door. Each night, she greeted me with a quick, *Entre*.

I was clumsy at first. Over anxious. A rushed lover. But the Queen taught me patience. Taught me how to wait. How to let the feelings build up inside of me.

The longer you wait, the bigger it is, she said.

I learned how to tickle her thighs, how to lick with precision, how to touch her nipples so they rose up under my fingers. How to use words to draw the wetness from her. How to crush my palm between her legs at just the right moment. The Queen's body was like a violin—she had not an extra pinch of fat on her. She was fine-boned and swan-necked. Yet, she gloried in my bigness—loved to sink her small hands into my breasts, to squeeze my stomach, to clutch my buttocks.

Mon dieu! she said. To have such flesh!

I learned other things with her. How to sleep next to another person. How to *really* sleep. To let go of my thoughts and exist solely as a body. At night, I was no more than the arms that held her, the legs that pressed against her. If I tried to move away from her in the night, she would cling onto me. And I was glad for it. I never wanted to leave her, not even for a moment.

Still. I worried we would be discovered. Wouldn't the King come some night, knocking on her door?

If he wants me, he sends a little note, she said. He never comes in here. Besides, I told him that I am suffering from an angry infection of the cunt. It will be weeks before he tries to lie with me again.

The other ladies-in-waiting did not mention my new status, nor the fact that I never slept in our chamber anymore. But the rift was plain. Ursuline curtseyed to me whenever I crossed her. Tamor whinnied like a horse in heat when I came near.

In the end, they dropped me entirely. My once-sisters. They no longer told me about their love affairs, or kissed my cheeks, or belched in front of me. But I was too full of love to mourn the loss. Then one morning, as I unfolded my dress, a dead rat rolled out from the pleats.

Laughter broke out behind me, but when I turned, the culprit was gone.

A week later, as I stood at the top of the stairs, rough hands shoved me in the back. I tripped down the spiral and landed on my face. Split my bottom lip and blackened both eyes.

When I went to the Queen's chamber that night, she cried, *ma chérie!* What's happened to you?

I told her I'd tripped, but she narrowed her eyes. Led me by the arm into the room where the lady's maids were having their tea. Ursuline was standing in the middle, rolling her eyes and thrusting her hips. When the Queen clapped her hands, she bowed her head.

Bonsoir, she said in a musical voice. I have something to say. If anyone lays a hand on this girl, she said, nodding at me, I will have your lips sliced off and your nipples cut out. I will have your throat slit. Then I will see you buried in the rose garden. *Comprenez-vous?*

Ursuline stared at her, mouth agape.

Trés bon, said the Queen. Good night, you little whores!

I had never been in love before, and had no idea how crazy it could make you. During the days, my eyes blurred with long-ing. I always wanted her, even when I was hard-used between the legs. I stared at myself in mirrors and did not recognize the feverish creature who looked back at me. I became dangerously careless—crashed into noblemen in the hall, kicked nosy palace dogs under the table, ate triple helpings at dinner. When my bodice became too tight, I tore out the seams.

Nights after making love, we would stay up until dawn, blood-flushed and curled toward each other like horns. The Queen told me stories about the monkey she'd had as a child, the antics of her deranged aunt, how she'd visited the seashore and seen a squid leap from the waves.

Tell me about your lovers, I said.

Why? she asked, lip twitching. Do you wish to suffer?

I want to know everything about you.

None of them are worth a pinch of you, she said, squeezing the flesh of my hip. With the others, I never lost my head.

And with me?

With you, I have no head at all. Sometimes I fear I will lose my heart.

But that's terrible, I said.

Why? she asked, kissing my nose. As long as you are there to hold it for me?

On the first night of Spring, the castle held a masked ball. The Queen ordered the lady's maids to be dressed as pigs for my amusement. Their masks were made of real bits of swine slaugh-tered for the feast. Wrinkled snouts and shrunken ears were nailed onto wooden masks. How we laughed to see Yvonne gag at the smell of putrid flesh! And at Ursuline, who shrieked each time she glimpsed her stiff corkscrew tail.

I came as Artemis, in an emerald dress with gold vines thread-ed down the bodice. A mask made of tiny brown feathers, and a golden arrow strapped to my back.

The Queen was Helen of Troy. She wore a thick cream-colored gown with a frothy neckline like breaking waves. A collar of tiny golden apples. Her black hair scandalously loose around her shoulders.

We smiled at each other as we danced with our partners. She

with the King, me with a young knight with violet pustules.

When the King returned to his seat, the Queen took me by the waist.

What are you doing? I hissed.

I could smell the wine on her breath as she swung me in arcs across the dance floor. Our skirts rustled together like frenzied bed sheets. We danced one song, then another. As we turned past the banquet table, the King glared at me over his wine.

People are staring, I said.

They're so drunk, they won't be able to find their own asses, said the Queen.

After another song, I pled exhaustion. The Queen relinquished me and gave my buttocks a sharp squeeze. I turned, but she was already gone, floating into the open arms of a beetle-browed duke.

You are a very spirited dancer, said a voice behind me.

I turned and saw the King. He held out a limp hand and I kissed his knuckle.

And pray, what are you dressed as? he said. A nymph? A fairy?

A hunter, I said.

Not very womanly, he remarked.

I hunted back in my own country, sire.

Ah—and what did you hunt?

Wolves. Ermine. Men who annoyed me.

He snorted. But then the Queen glided past us, and his smile fell.

She should not dance like that, he said. It rattles the eggs. No wonder I have no heirs. That woman's womb is a veritable snake pit.

I narrowed my eyes. Your lord will forgive me, I said. But I do believe you have a bit of egg in your beard! I bent forward and plucked a piece of white from the dark tangles.

There, I said. All clean!

He stared at me, mouth open. I gave him a toothy smile, curtseyed, and walked off.

Two days after the ball, I was sewing in my chamber when a servant knocked on the door. He handed me a folded piece of parchment. I read the slanted writing—the King expected me in his bed the following night.

I let the note flutter to my feet.

At that moment, Joselyn appeared in the doorway. She glanced at me, then the note.

Ahh, she said, her face splitting into a smile. So finally it's *your* turn.

I stared at her, unable to speak.

Try not to think about it too much, she said, thrusting out a hip and leaning against the door. And don't worry—I'll draw a bath for you afterward. We don't want you getting blood on the Queen's nice sheets.

Later that night, I showed the Queen the note. She glanced down at the broken seal, then got up and began to pace the room. She walked back and forth across the animal skins, then paused before the crystal window.

So, she whispered at last. He is not as stupid as I thought.

I stood up, but she held up a long-boned hand.

He'll take everything from me in the end. He doesn't want me to bear a son—just to die of misery.

But what can we *do*? I asked.

There's nothing to do. You must go to him.

I began to speak, but she gave me a brutal look. Child, don't you know he'll kill you if you don't?

Then I'll die, I said.

Fool, she whispered. Let us speak of it no more.

In her bed that night, I tried to hold her, but she slipped away from me. We slept apart for the first time. I lay awake, the five inches between us rising up like a trellised wall.

The next morning, I rose, dressed, and walked out of the castle. I met Tamor at the gates, talking breathily to a stable boy. When she saw me, she wagged her tongue.

I moved across the wet lawns, down a path to the entrance to the King's forest. Breathed in the smell of rotting bark and brackish moss. For the first time in months, I thought of Italy— of my brothers and their dirty little feet.

I walked and walked under the drapery of trees, past red mushrooms and floating moths. Finally, something made me stop. A clump of blue flowers growing at the base of a tree. I knew these flowers, though I had never seen them in this country. My Grandmother had told me about them. If you wanted to kill an enemy, you would place a whole blossom into their tea, and their insides would rot.

I plucked a single petal and pinched it between my fingers. Then, with a sigh, I placed it on my tongue and swallowed.

I made it back to the castle before the convulsions began. On the frigid stones of my chamber, I sprawled and retched into a basin. My skin turned yellow and broke out in a fine sweat. Shit funneled down my legs. In the end, Ursuline, who had squealed with laughter upon first finding me, knelt by my side.

What in God's name did you eat? she said.

When the King's servant came to collect me after dinner, he found me heaped on the floor, spitting bile. He gave me one disgusted look and left.

Soon, I had thrown up everything inside of me. My organs were scalded, my lips cracked, and I lost consciousness. I was vaguely aware of hands lifting me, then lowering me onto a soft bed. I had fevered dreams of severed ears and steaming organs and toads that spoke like little girls.

When I awoke hours later, the Queen's chamber was full of sun. The Queen was lying next to me, her face carved in anger.

Before she could question me, I told her what I'd done.

But *why*? she asked.

I couldn't go to him, I said simply.

Le fou! Don't you know he'll take you the moment you're better?

I gave her a weak smile. There are more flowers. Now we know a single petal won't kill you.

She shook her head. Her eyes crowded with tears. You could have *died*, she said.

I lifted a limp hand and touched the side of her head. She took it and kissed my wrist.

After a long silence, she whispered, Don't you know that if you died, I would have to follow you?

It took me a full month to recover from the petal's poison. For a time, I could take no food or water without retching. The flesh

I'd gained in the past months fell away from me. I became a pale creature, all bones and hollows. But when the sickness finally abated—when I was weak, but no longer in danger—the Queen and I had beautiful days. We stayed in bed, drinking dandelion tea, exchanging tales of our lives. She played the guitar for me and made up stories. She massaged my bones with lavender salve. Brushed my hair. Dressed and undressed me.

Who knew that I would make such a wonderful lady's maid? she said.

But she was right about the King. A few days after I returned to court, a small note came by way of a servant. The King, demanding my company the following night.

The Queen and I sat together in bed, the note between us.

I thought I could let him have you, she said softly. I thought I could bear it.

And now? I said.

She combed a hand through her hair. I saw the strands of silver among the dark coils, the crackle of veins beneath her temple. For once she looked her age.

You have to go, she said.

No, I said, sitting up. You can't make me.

I'm the Queen, she said with a small smile. Of course I can.

I'll kill him, I said. Put the flower in his wine. Or stab him in the heart, I don't care.

She laughed a high, tinkling laugh and touched my cheek.

Oh, *ma poule*, she said. I will never recover from you.

The next morning, the Queen arranged for me to be smuggled away with a load of carpets. A giant man with a hatchet face would take me to a ship, which would sail me across the ocean. I had a stash of jewels sewn into the inside of my skirt. This same man would accompany me to the colonies. He would make sure that I did not get killed, or worse, try to come back.

I walked to the gate with the Queen, concealed under a plain brown cloak. I had refused to speak or even look at her since she'd told me her plan. She had silenced my arguments by saying, in a calm voice, that if I did not obey, she would have me killed and buried in the rose garden.

We walked in silence. At the edge of the forest, the wagon

was waiting, the hatchet-faced man at the reins. The Queen gripped my face and forced me to look at her. I clamped my mouth shut and closed my eyes. She sighed. Lay a kiss between my eyebrows.

This is not goodbye, she said. I will come for you.

When? I sneered. How long do you expect me to wait?

She opened her mouth, then closed it.

I wrenched away from her, climbed into the back of the wagon, and sat atop a stack of carpets. The man slapped the horses with the reigns. We began to trundle away.

The Queen held out her hand. I looked at it and spit on the ground.

The port city was a filthy place—streets clotted with half-dried shit, cats batting at dead pigeons. The hatchet-faced-man booked us a room at an inn. We would sail the next morning for America. He assured me that life was good in the colonies, that I would have no trouble finding a man. He was kind, and I felt badly for what I had to do. When his head was turned, I dropped a blue petal into his cup of evening ale.

An hour later, he was writhing on the floor, spewing vomit clear across the room. I said that I was sorry.

I went to town. Traded my jewels for silver, then bought a horse, a knife, a rope, a bow, and a quiver of arrows. I bought men's clothes and a long cape. I cut my hair and threw the locks into a puddle of mud.

I rode my horse for hours before I reached a shaggy hill with a small cottage on top. The old farmer who lived there was awed by the sum of silver I offered him. In return, he left me a large stock of millet, dried beans, salted beef, and barley wine.

When I first bought the cottage, a few rogue vines were creeping up the sides. By the end of the Spring rains, the vines had taken over the whole house, closing it in beneath an emerald jacket.

On the northern wall of the cottage, a window looked out over the valley. If I peered directly downward, I could see a house at the foot of the hill. A stone manor, its garden lined with cherry trees. In the mornings, I watched smoke curl from the crown of chimneys. If I listened, I could hear the voices of young girls caught on the breeze. Girls whose voices were changing, thickening, their songs growing louder, more beautiful, more strange.

I hunted boar in the early hours of morning. The rest of the day, I stood by the window, looking down, watching. Waiting.

All those hours, all those days. A month passed, then another. Soon, half a year had gone.

Waiting is not such a terrible way to spend a life.

And then one day I saw a woman approach the manor. She had black hair piled on top of her head, and wore a ribbon over her eyes. I watched her knock and enter. I heard the high-pitched cries of the girls.

I crept down the hill and plunged an arrow into the ground by the gate. Then I returned to the cottage and sat in the darkness.

Hours later, there was a knock at the door. It was soft, unsure.

Ma poule? said the voice. Is it you?

I sat perfectly still. I closed my eyes. I waited for the door to open.

RACHEL ENGELMAN spent the last eight years in Argentina where she founded The Walrus School, a school of creative writing and literature workshops. Her autobiographical story was published and translated in Clarín, Argentina's largest newspaper. She was recently a finalist for The 2017 Crazyhorse Fiction Prize, and shortlisted for The Masters Review Winter Short Story Award. She is now an MFA fellow at the Michener Center for Writers in Austin, Texas. This is her first fiction publication.

Migrations

Michele Host

The agency liked to tell prospective hires that the most important qualification for becoming a Child Protective Services worker was loving children. If Nikki did the hiring, she'd say the most important thing was the ability to wait. She'd waited at shelters, at hospitals, and in courtrooms. She'd waited on subway platforms to help mothers carry strollers up stairways, in dank project hallways to dole out cleaning supplies, and in principals' offices to get copies of transcripts. She'd waited for her supervisors to approve requests for MetroCards so that parents who lived in Canarsie could visit their kids who were placed in Woodside, and for grouchy nuns to give her bags of clothes for kids who'd been evicted. And when Nikki woke up every day, she waited to breathe until she checked the headlines on her phone.

Nikki had been waiting outside Part 10 for an hour when she realized her case probably wasn't getting called. The judge's court attorney had promised that her case would be called right after lunch. "We'll be in and out in ten minutes," he said, heavy glasses sliding down his nose as he flipped from file to file. "2:00 time certain. Trial discharge. No problem."

As the lawyers and social workers shuffled out of the part's windowless conference room that day, Nikki had allowed herself to be optimistic. Visits were going well. Social workers had visited the mother's new apartment in a supportive housing complex, and one told Nikki that the kids' bedrooms were not only clean and full of furniture, but covered with movie posters from recent Disney movies. The mother's new psychiatrist submitted a report confirming that she was attending appointments and compliant on her meds after her old doctor switched her doses every other week as a part of a research study. (The wild pharmacological swings had caused her to perform a striptease on a very crowded 4 train. While singing "The Star-Spangled Banner.")

When Nikki got to court in the morning, she had seen the court attorney in the foyer, still in his commuting sneakers, flirting with a court officer. He grabbed Nikki's arm as she walked by and signaled for her to remove her headphones.

"The judge is ready to send those kids home on your 2:00," he said. Nikki half-smiled, not wanting to seem too eager. But all morning she'd carried hope in her heart the way she'd once held a baby chicken in the cage of her hands. And when she saw the mother in the waiting area at 10:00—four full hours before her case was scheduled—Nikki almost ran over to hug her before remembering that they were technically opposing parties.

But then the kids' lawyer wasn't outside the courtroom at 2:00. A court officer strode around the waiting area, yelling "Parties on Patterson. Patterson. Parties on Patterson," before slowly shaking his head and disappearing behind the metal courtroom door. When the kids' lawyer finally arrived, she made a show of running from the elevator. ("Mani-pedi," she whispered to Nikki, leaning in so close that Nikki could smell the fruit basket of her shampoo. "I love that place on Church Street but they take forever.") By then, the judge had already called her 2:15 trial ahead of them, so they all sat down to wait.

The waiting area was overwhelmingly brown. Brown as corduroy, as mud, as brownies, as Nikki's darkest-skinned uncle. Beige tile, wooden benches for the endless supplicants, brown walls. The outside of the family court building had originally been shiny black. At some point, someone in city government realized that an onyx cube might be inhospitable to children in distress, and the facade was lightened. To gray. Either way, the decision to make the interior areas feel like a 1970s leisure suit was one of the things Nikki pondered during her waits. She eventually concluded that when the building went up, the city had a surplus of brown stuff in a warehouse somewhere. So that's what the poor children of Manhattan got.

Nikki created a miniature office for herself on her wooden pew as she waited, pulling out her laptop to enter progress notes and send emails. As more people filed in for the afternoon docket, the high-ceilinged waiting area got louder and hotter. Outside, summer had made a splashy return. Even though the trees had exploded in yellows and reds, women were bare-legged, crunching on fallen leaves with open-toed sandals. But the courthouse's air-conditioning was already off for the season. The air was thick with heat and the fish sauce funk of someone's banh mi sandwich.

A little girl smiled at Nikki from an umbrella stroller. Kids tended to like Nikki; her coworkers said it was because Nikki was so short that kids thought she was one of them. When Nikki smiled back at the girl, she saw movement near the leg of her yellow shorts. A cockroach crawled out, climbed down the leg of the stroller, and skittered across the room.

Nikki's phone vibrated in her bag. When she pulled it out, its screen was a funny page of emoji: beer steins, martini glasses, smiley faces, hearts. It was her roommate, Marcus, commanding her to meet him at a party in Williamsburg after work. Nikki sighed. She was not dressed for a party. Her gray pants and light-blue button-down signaled someone who wanted to put on pajamas and sit on the couch. Marcus had mocked her outfit when they were getting ready for work, saying that all she needed was a pair of orthopedic shoes to begin a new career as a dental assistant.

Her phone vibrated again, and she ignored it. A janitor sloshed by, the artificial lemon smell of his cleaning liquid scalding Nikki's nose. Why was institutional floor soap always lemon scented? Why not eucalyptus, or lavender? Swearing under her breath, Nikki looked across the room at the mother. She had a magazine in her lap, but she wasn't reading it. Their eyes locked, and the mother sat up straighter, as if she could prove something to Nikki with her posture.

The mother's social worker felt her shift and put his arm around her. He was a tall, curly-haired guy who favored shawl-collared sweaters with wooden buttons. Nikki suspected that he became a social worker to pick up women, a suspicion she might have felt guilty about if he hadn't rubbed her thigh once when they were discussing a teenage dad's pot habit. Wandering hands could be excused at a bar, but when they were discussing how a stressed-out homeless kid could get his baby back, flirting was just wrong.

Behind her, a door banged open. Heads turned throughout the waiting area. It was the court officer who reminded Nikki of a high school football player, with a buzzcut and puffy cheeks that were cherubic or dissolute, depending on the light. He surveyed the room, clipboard in hand like a coach choosing his starting line-up. Nikki knew that if he was coming out alone, that wasn't a good sign. That meant the trial was still going on.

"If you've got a case in Part 10 today, it's getting adjourned," he droned, giving away his sense of self-importance with the lift of his chest. "Approach and I'll give you your adjournment date." The waiting area exhaled in a collective sigh before people pulled out their phones and day planners. From one corner, a high-pitched wail.

Nikki winced and looked at the mother. She was standing up, clearly trying to get to the court officer. The social worker was trying to block her route, and the mother was darting from side to side to get past him. They looked like a gif of two people trying to pass in a narrow hallway, stuck on repeat. Nikki ran over.

"I'm so sorry about the adjournment, Ms. Patterson," she said, holding out one hand like she was stopping traffic. "It has nothing to do with you and the kids, you know that, right?" The mother was still shuffling from one foot to the other, but with less forward momentum. Nikki tried to meet her eyes, but Ms. Patterson could have been watching tennis, her eyes darted back and forth so quickly.

"Your case is getting moved because the judge is busy, not because you aren't doing great. Because you are. You're doing everything we've asked you to do." Nikki paused, and Ms. Patterson tried to push past her. But Nikki stepped to the right at the same time, which brought them nose-to-nose, like prize fighters or lovers.

Nikki leaned in and whispered in Ms. Patterson's ear. "If you carry on in front of that court officer, he'll tell the judge. And the judge will tell everybody else. And it will be like all that work never happened." With that, Ms. Patterson went slack, like a rubber band pulled to its limit and released. She sat back down on the bench and put her head in her hands.

"Do you have children?" she asked, without looking up. Nikki sighed and looked at the splotchy ceiling.

"No, ma'am, I don't."

Ms. Patterson looked up, face striped with the shine of her tears. "So that's why you got a job taking other people's children?"

The social worker leaned in, about to speak, but Nikki waved him back. "I know this is a hard time," Nikki said. "I'll leave you two alone. But let him get the adjournment slip for you. And if you want extra visits with the kids before the next court date, we can do that. Just call me."

*   *   *

People who don't want guests wearing shoes in their apartments shouldn't throw parties, Nikki thought. She and Marcus had pounded on the buzzer for ten minutes before someone heard them, and after they'd climbed six flights of stairs carpeted in what appeared to be bellybutton lint, they shouldered their way through the door only to stumble on a tangle of shoes. Of course, Marcus just kicked off his loafers and plunged his way into the party, leaving Nikki to glare at the "Shoes Off Please!" sign taped on the wall by herself. She had a hole in her right sock. The urge to stomp down the stairs rose in her throat. Instead, Nikki picked up Marcus's shoes, removed her own, and tucked both pairs off to one side of the entryway so that they wouldn't get lost.

Nikki shuffled through a long hallway, her big toe poking out of her sock. A woman in a leopard-print blouse tottered past on red heels, clearly having ignored the shoe instructions, and she tossed her hair with such vigor that strands of it got stuck in Nikki's lip gloss. Nikki stuck her tongue out like a cat trying to get rid of a hairball, realizing that none of the people at the party had probably ever thought of Manhattan Family Court. Or of the people who ended up there. Which made her more depressed than accidentally eating a stranger's hair.

Finally Nikki found the alcohol, poured herself a plastic cup of something red, and leaned against a wall. As she sipped, her wine reminded her of cherry cough syrup, and she realized that she should have kept searching the table for white instead of settling for a bottle of red with a drawing of a penguin on the label.

Nikki contemplated a group of family photos on the wall. Judging by the very different families in the frames—a group of five redheads in matching navy v-neck sweaters, two Korean women cooing over a bassinet, and a throng of blondes in ski gear with peeling noses—at least three people lived in the apartment. Nikki realized that she and Marcus didn't have any family photographs hanging in their place. Just a snapshot on the fridge of the two of them at the Rockaways eating tacos.

"Where are you from?" a guy standing across from her asked. He had been leaning against the wall for a while, and she'd assumed he was waiting for the bathroom. Nikki wondered if he thought she was staring at him when she was ogling the photographs.

"Where do I live or where am I from?"

Nikki's words, delivered with the raised left eyebrow she'd been practicing in the mirror since she was twelve, prompted him to execute a dorky slide-step across the hallway. He had an orange button-down shirt on, which was endearingly formal in a sea of men wearing ironic t-shirts. Below his dark jeans Nikki saw navy argyle socks with a vein of orange running through the pattern. He was someone who took some degree of effort with his life. Or at least with his hosiery.

"Both," he said, and Nikki realized that he was so much taller than her that she needed to back up to talk to his face instead of his chest. His face and forearms were freckled in a way that reminded her of the Future Farmers of America members from high school, even though she knew the sprinkling of melanin was probably just a result of pick-up soccer or weekends upstate.

As they talked, Nikki reminded herself that this was a Brooklyn party, so the guy flirting with her probably was not a serial killer. Some of the people eating olives and pointedly looking at the bookshelves might not be vegetarians, and some of them might not have locked down their positions on charter schools, but they were probably all well-intentioned, earnest, food co-op patronizing people. Social workers. Programmers. Bloggers. Development aides. If there were finance people somewhere in the two-bedroom apartment, they were only working at Morgan Stanley until they could pay off their student loans. Or their kid brothers' student loans.

"I live in Gowanus but I grew up in Wisconsin," Nikki finally said.

"There are no black people in Wisconsin," he scoffed, with a curl to his thin upper lip that revealed he thought he was being edgy. Nikki tried to remember who Marcus knew at this party as she considered whether or not she should dump her wine on the guy's head.

"You're looking at a black person from Wisconsin," she said flatly. "Born and bred."

He arched an eyebrow above his glasses and tipped his beer bottle at her.

"If you're from Wisconsin," he said, "shouldn't you be drinking Milwaukee's Best? No king of beers for you?"

Again, the urge to leave. If Nikki had wanted to keep talking, she could have told him that there's more to Wisconsin than beer. Described skipping class in high school to go to Brewers games. Told stories about Ivanhoe; how families making contingency plans after the Chicago riots bought eighty-three acres next to a lake ringed with rushes and cattails. How Cab Calloway blew his horn to open the pavilion where she and her cousins had played tag. Or she could have talked about Wisconsin food. Her longest romantic relationship in New York had begun on the strength of her taxonomy of the fried food offerings at the Walworth County Fair.

But she didn't. She was ready to get on the train, so she drained her cup and put it on a stack of magazines.

"I don't like beer," she said as she walked away. Which was true. She never had.

Of course, Marcus was in the center of the largest conversational amoeba in the living room. She touched his arm, enjoying the familiar softness of his favorite cashmere sweater while being irritated with him for wasting it on a smoky party.

"There you are!" he said, kissing Nikki's cheek. "Excuse me," he said to his audience, "I must debrief with my roommate."

"You're going to have to take that sweater right to the dry cleaner tomorrow," Nikki said as they turned to one another. Marcus rolled his eyes.

"What do you want to do?" he asked. He gestured toward the food table, with its gingham tablecloth and Jenga-stacked boxes of water crackers. "Want anything to eat?"

"They could have at least put the hummus in a bowl," Nikki said, eyeing a tub of custardy gloop. The salsa was also still in its jar, pieces of chip already drowning in an acid bath.

"What they need is some microwave popcorn," Marcus answered. "They have a microwave, they should use it."

During their first week of college, Marcus had stumbled into their dorm lounge on his way home from a party. Nikki was burrowed into the decomposing couch, watching *The Thorn Birds* and hiding from her roommate, who spent every night murmuring to her hometown boyfriend on the phone and burning her arm with a cigarette lighter. Marcus sank into the couch next to her.

"I love this show so much," he said. "Priests and Australian accents. What could be better? You got any snacks?"

Nikki passed him her bag of microwave popcorn, and that was that.

In Williamsburg, two guys who had been jousting over whose iPhone had better music were now hooking up a karaoke machine.

"I don't think I can handle karaoke," Nikki said. "Can we go?"

Marcus sighed. "The story of my life," he said.

Later, after she and Marcus had waited for a G train, and he had whined about her making him live in a neighborhood that regularly required them to take the G train, they were finally home. They genuflected to the statue of the Virgin Mary in their building's yard, which they did whenever they got home late, and shushed one another up the stairs, not wanting to wake the two generations of Marinos on the first and second floors. When they had dumped their bags and taken off their shoes, Nikki debated drinking a glass of wine that would turn into vinegar by morning. She settled for eating a bowl of strawberry ice cream.

Once Marcus had closed the door to his bedroom, Nikki

folded down the futon and got into bed. But she wasn't able to sleep. The laughter of people walking to the restaurant down the street sounded sinister as it drifted through the window, and the wooden bar in the middle of the futon mattress felt like it was going to impale one of her kidneys. She tried to imagine that she could hear the canal a few blocks away. They had moved to Gowanus because Nikki wanted to be near water, but you could never really hear the canal. You could only smell it. Green, muddy, and still, it only moved when acted upon. Like when an errant dolphin or seal got lost and swam upstream. Occasionally she saw a few ducks when she walked across the Third Street Bridge, and she always wondered if they might have flown from Wisconsin.

Nikki rearranged herself on the futon so that she was lying across it horizontally. One of the blessings of being short, she thought. As she wrestled with the top sheet, she thought back to the weekends when her grandma would wake her up early to go and find her mom. She'd pull Nikki out of bed, buckle her into the passenger seat of her Monte Carlo, and they'd rumble through Ivanhoe. People were always coming back from an overnight shift somewhere, and the cars would have to lean around one another to pass on the narrow roads. Nikki would say the street names to herself as they drove along. Crispus Attucks Drive. Phillis Wheatley Drive. Charles Young Drive. Tuskegee Drive. One morning, when she was nine, she asked her grandmother who Phillis Wheatley was.

"Aren't they teaching you that at school?" she asked back. Nikki's grandma was always answering questions with questions.

Nikki said no, and her grandma's hands tightened around the steering wheel. The following Monday, Nikki didn't take the bus to school. Her grandma drove her, walked her inside, and turned at the principal's office, shooing Nikki off to her classroom.

Usually on their weekend trips to Milwaukee, Nikki would fall back asleep, at least for a little while. Sometimes she'd wake up in time to beg her grandma to pull over in Mukwonago so they could split an enormous muffin from the Elegant Farmer. Grandma would always sigh and signal for the exit, even though the workers followed them around the store like they were wearing prison jumpsuits.

More often the smell of hops woke Nikki up as they drove into the city. They'd get near the Marquette sign, and that sour, yeasty odor would pulse through the car. They weren't always smelling the hops from the factory, though. Wherever they found Nikki's mother, if they found her, she was usually surrounded by beer cans. Nikki's memories of her mother were all shiny with aluminum. Once, Marcus dragged her to an exhibit at the Brooklyn Museum by an African artist whose art was made of cans and foil and pull tabs. Strolling through the galleries, Nikki kept expecting to see her mother curled up asleep on one of the sculptures, even though she'd been dead since Nikki was in high school. Froze to death. Went outside, drunk, in a blizzard. Sat down in one of those Milwaukee alley yards. It was a party and everyone assumed she went home with somebody else. They didn't find her until the snow melted.

Nikki eventually managed to get to sleep, and by the time she woke up the next morning Marcus was already gone. He'd left her some tea, though, in the insulated cup that she took with her in the field. She made herself toast and groaned when she saw that her first home visit was for an educational neglect case. There was almost always something going on in ed neglect cases besides the kid missing school. If a kid was missing so much school that somebody called it in, his mom had also forgotten to get him his medication. Or was smoking too much weed to get the medication. Or had grabbed the kid on the arm so hard that there was a bruise. Sometimes the kid really was just sick—like the time a school secretary failed to tell a principal that a third-grader had been diagnosed with leukemia, and Nikki had to visit the kid at Mount Sinai to confirm that he wasn't skipping school.

Once, she went to a house—an entire brownstone—in Brooklyn Heights, on Pineapple Street. The mom glided to the door in an embroidered caftan and told Nikki that the kids hadn't been to school for three weeks because their au pair had gone back to Barcelona. "They're just too emotional to leave the house," she said, stroking the silky gray cat tucked in the crook of her arm. When the mom left the living room to make tea, the five-year-old tugged on Nikki's jacket.

"You wanna make pictures?"

Nikki almost missed it. She crouched down, looked in the girl's eyes, and was about to talk about crayons and colored pencils. Something made her ask, "What kind of pictures?"

The little girl pushed her tangled hair away from her face. "Special pictures."

Nikki held out her hand. "Show me where you make the special pictures," she said. The little girl took her hand and led her up the stairs, where a back room had been rigged up like a photography studio. Cameras worth more than a month's rent, screens, lights, the works. And piles of tiny lingerie. In a pink toy laundry basket, a set of handcuffs. Dildos. Turns out the dad had lost his job and they were streaming porn of the kids to pay the mortgage.

As Nikki boarded the B65 bus, sweaty from jogging to Atlantic after waiting for a B103 that never came, she had no reason to expect a scenario like that on her morning trip to New York Avenue. She tried to let her mind wander with the music on her headphones, but she kept returning to the case file in her bag. There were three kids in the house. Two in elementary school, ages nine and six, and a three-year-old. The two oldest had perfect attendance but didn't show up again after summer break. No one thought to call it in until the oldest boy's teacher from the year before ran into the mom in a bodega. The teacher said the mom dropped a six-pack of toilet paper, she was so nervous. Then a neighbor called the hotline a few days later. Charisse, her name was. She said she still saw the parents coming and going, the dad to his job at the post office and the mom to the supermarket, but she never saw the kids anymore, and the blinds were always down. "I'm not nosy," Charisse said. "I'm just worried."

Nikki wanted to say, "This is New York, we're all nosy." But she didn't.

Nikki was half expecting the neighbor to be on the stoop when she arrived. But the only people around were a bunch of guys waiting for the bus at the end of the block. The family lived on the bottom two floors of a brownstone. Not one of the ones that had been flipped and rehabbed, with the cash practically sliding out of the double-plate windows, but not one of the ones with cracked sidewalks and missing bricks either. The

Harris place was just solid. Window boxes that had recently been tended and prepared for winter. But like Charisse said, the shades were all drawn.

Nikki rang the buzzer, and she thought she saw a small hand at the front window. Then she heard footsteps. The door opened slowly, and only far enough for Nikki to see a woman she assumed must be Adelphi Harris behind a chain lock that remained fastened. The architectural snap of Mrs. Harris's posture made Nikki try to roll her shoulders back, and she almost choked herself with the strap of her messenger bag. Even with the door chained, Nikki recognized that Mrs. Harris was church people, as her grandma would say. Mrs. Harris was at least five inches taller than Nikki, and her clothes were as crisp as her posture. Nikki suspected that if she could see under Mrs. Harris's white button-down, even her bra would have been ironed.

Mrs. Harris did not say hello, so Nikki spoke first. "Hi, are you Mrs. Harris? My name is Nicole Green, and I'm with the Administration for Children's Services."

Before Nikki could even get the last consonant out, the door slammed. Enough locks shoved and clicked to protect the US Mint, the recipe for Coke, and the crown jewels of Europe. Nikki buzzed again.

"Mrs. Harris, I just want to talk to you. And see the kids."

Silence. Again.

"Mrs. Harris?"

"It's Dr. Harris."

Nikki exhaled before resting her forehead gently on the door. Nothing set a home visit off on the wrong foot like getting a name or a title wrong.

"I apologize, Dr. Harris," Nikki said. "But you've still got to let me in. You're not going to like who comes next." Nikki wasn't shouting, but she was getting louder. "If I don't see those kids, I call the police."

That was the magic word, as it often was. The door opened, and Nikki stumbled into the dark. Somehow, even though the front windows were closed, the house wasn't stuffy. The baby fingers of light that slid in around the edges of the blinds didn't catch any dust. And then Nikki heard it, the sweet hum of central air. Not a sound she heard often on home visits.

Dr. Harris clicked through her lock routine again, entered something into a security key pad, and looked at Nikki. Dr. Harris's hair was pulled into a twist, and she wore pearls on each ear. Her white shirt was tucked into a pair of tweed pants that made Nikki think of Sherlock Holmes. An organization unit on the wall rivaled anything Nikki had seen in magazines. There was a bench for putting on shoes, two rows of hooks on the wall, and canvas pockets for mail. On the hooks, canvas totes from Trader Joe's and the Brooklyn Public Library. Two pairs of adult sneakers. No kids' shoes.

"The children are reading in the library," Dr. Harris said, staring in Nikki's eyes. "Shall we?"

Nikki followed her through the living room, walking slowly so that she could take it in. It was every middle American's fantasy of what it might be like to live in New York. The windows swept almost to the ceiling, framed in thick wooden beams. An enormous fireplace was topped by an oil painting of three women, arms linked in an embrace. On the other walls, books. Novels and art books and history books, all mismatched and broken-in and read. Nikki found herself longing to grab a book and lie down on the brown leather couch to read for a while.

In the one break in the bookshelves where most people would put a television, there was an oversized family photograph. Mr. Harris was even taller than Dr. Harris, his arm around her and a smile so wide Nikki wondered if the photographer had told a joke before taking the picture.Or maybe he was gently making fun of Dr. Harris for making all of them wear white button-down shirts for the photograph. Maybe Adelphi Harris wears only white button-downs, Nikki thought.

In the kitchen, Nikki smelled something rich and meaty in the oven. Maybe lasagna. On the kitchen island, bowls of bananas and apples. But besides some drawings on the refrigerator, there were no signs of children. No sippy cups, no stray toys. It was bright; sliding glass doors opened up onto a small yard surrounded by a high fence. Nikki's stomach began to twist. What if this perfect woman with her perfect house had done something extremely imperfect with her children?

They approached a small room behind the kitchen, and Nikki finally spotted the children. Involuntarily, she exhaled. The two boys were sprawled on an overstuffed couch, reading, and the little girl was on the floor wrestling with a stuffed dog. A white cat walked the back of the couch like a balance beam.

"Children," Dr. Harris said. "Stand up and say hello to—," she looked at Nikki and smiled for the first time, but only with her mouth. Not with her eyes.

"Nicole."

She turned back to the children. The two oldest were now standing, hands behind their backs.

"Nicole," she said. "Connor's teacher from last year, Miss Delia, sent her to check up on us." Nikki was impressed that Dr. Harris explained Nikki's sudden appearance in a way so close to the truth.

"Pleased to meet you," Connor said, and he stepped forward to shake Nikki's hand. His brother stood quietly next to him.

"This is Derrick," Connor said, "and this is Tia."

Derrick just nodded, and Tia was absorbed in putting her foot behind her ear. "Can I talk to them for a few minutes alone?" Nikki asked.

Dr. Harris crossed her arms and her lips tightened. "I'll be right in the kitchen," she said. Mostly to Connor, who nodded. Tia started to wail when Dr. Harris stepped out, and Nikki dug *The Runaway Bunny* out of her bag.

"We already have that one," Derrick said.

The wailing started to sound more like a siren, and Nikki could feel Dr. Harris in the kitchen behind her. Connor picked up *Listen to My Trumpet!* and wrestled Tia onto his lap. As he pulled his little boy voice deep into his chest for the bespectacled elephant and squealed as the pig, his brother leaned against him. Sitting criss-cross applesauce, just like them, Nikki felt her shoulders relax.

"Did you come from outside?" Derrick asked when he finished reading.

"Yes, I did."

He pulled at the hem of his gray t-shirt. "I like outside."

"We go outside," Connor said.

"Only out there," Derrick tilted his head toward the sliding door. "Not to the playground. Or the museum. Or the store."

"Tell me what you like to do outside," Nikki said. And with

that, it all came out. Derrick described sitting at the counter of his favorite diner, eating doughnuts with sprinkles, and watching the Mets. Which made Connor think of little league, and the home run he hit, and how he didn't get to play this year.

"I never got to do geography," Derrick said. "Third grade is when you start doing geography."

"I even miss shoe shopping," Connor said, eyeing the pile of flip-flops and sneakers near the door.

"How do you get your shoes now?" Nikki asked. From below the longest eyelashes she'd ever seen outside of a baby animal video, Connor looked at her like she was dumb as a sack of hammers.

"Zappos."

The only time they got outside now was in the little yard, they told her. They played freeze tag and tossed around a football, but there wasn't enough space for baseball. They showed Nikki workbooks that they worked on with their mom, and described days more academically rigorous than her high school AP classes. Nikki studied the room, which had more bookshelves on the walls. On the few exposed spaces, there were framed photographs, but not of family. Of Flo-Jo. Of Doctor King. Obama. Neil deGrasse Tyson. Nikki asked the kids the obvious question. Why did they think their mother was keeping them at home?

"It's safer this way," Connor said, as Derrick nodded. "Until we move. When we move, it will all be different."

Nikki left the room with Connor and Derrick playing a heated game of Connect-4 and Tia banging on a toy piano. Dr. Harris was sitting at the kitchen island, using a shiny device to chop perfect piles of carrot, celery, and cucumber sticks. She did not stop her chopping when Nikki entered the room, instead using her contraption to punctuate the conversation.

"They're the best, aren't they?" Chop.

"They're amazing," Nikki said.

"So you understand what I'm trying to do?" Chop.

If Nikki couldn't see that Dr. Harris was only chopping carrots, cucumbers, and celery, she would have thought she was chopping onions from the tears pooling at the corners of her eyes. Nikki couldn't remember her own mother ever chopping vegetables, she realized. The list of things Nikki could remember her mother doing was embarrassingly short, and did not include cooking. Most of her memories of her mother were backed up by photographs in her grandma's house. So Nikki suspected that she did not truly remember her mother decorating her big wheel for the 4th of July parade when she was three, or building a sand castle with her when she was four. She had just created the memories from the photographs in her grandma's collages.

There was one night she remembered without any photographic evidence. Nikki was riding in the passenger seat of her mother's silver-blue Eagle when she definitely should have been in a car seat in the back. They were driving near the big lake, and the smells of seaweed and diesel fuel from the motorboats filled the car. Her mother's eyes were hidden behind enormous sunglasses, but she was smiling and singing along to MacArthur Park on the radio. Nikki had a cone of custard, and she wanted to keep driving forever. Looking at Dr. Harris, Nikki wondered if she had ever untucked that white shirt and danced. You never could tell.

"If you wanted to homeschool them, all you had to do was submit the paperwork," Nikki said. "You just send a letter of intent to the Department of Education. And then—"

"I know that," Dr. Harris said, chopping harder and faster. "And then you send the IHIP plan with your syllabus and list of books. I wrote the letter back in May, and I have the plan all put together too."

"Why didn't you send it all in, then?" Nikki asked.

Dr. Harris finally stopped chopping. "Because homeschooling wasn't going to be enough. I have to get them out of here."

"Where will you go?"

Mrs. Harris smiled. With her straight, shiny teeth and her eyes. "Canada. Montreal. Safe and far away from here."

Nikki had never been to Canada, but she imagined it must be a lot like Wisconsin, except with mounties and universal health care. She walked over to the archway separating the kitchen from the library. Connor and Derrick were both reading now, feet-to-feet on the couch. Connor had the same old paperback copy of *My Side of the Mountain* that Nikki had bought at the library book sale for a nickel when she was nine, and Derrick was reading a Geronimo Stilton book.

"Haven't they made it harder for Americans to move to Canada?" Nikki asked.

Dr. Harris was still smiling. "I'm a cardiologist," she said. "The day after I sent my resume to a head-hunter up there, I had five interviews scheduled, and five days after I flew up there I had five job offers."

"Why Canada," Nikki asked as she drifted back into the middle of the kitchen. "Why not just leave the city?"

Dr. Harris frowned and started chopping again. "Five years ago, even three years ago, I could control everything," she said, celery sticks piling up in a stack. "Avoid this block, avoid this bus. Don't ever go to that bodega. Take the kids to school, pick them up right after. The neighborhood was getting better." She spoke softly but firmly, eyes periodically darting toward the children.

"Trayvon Martin was when things really started to get to me. One day my husband was walking Connor and Derrick home from a play date and they both had hoodies on. I ran up to them in the middle of the street and ripped the hoodies off. They both started to cry. I couldn't sleep. I worked fewer hours so I could take them to school, volunteer. I'd saved a lot, and my husband has good benefits so it was fine but. . .But it kept coming."

Dr. Harris's voice was trembling, and her hands were shaking so much that she had to stop chopping. She turned away, and Nikki didn't know what to do. At past home visits, she'd seen everything from a pile of dead rats under a crib to a five-year-old so malnourished he looked like a stick figure, but something about seeing this capable woman in tears was unsettling. Nikki walked to the sliding door and looked at the yard. In the corner, there was a rosebush, as well as three wire cages awaiting tomato plants. The wooden fence surrounding the yard was so high that they could have been anywhere.

Behind her, Dr. Harris blew her nose, and Nikki turned around. "Then Tamir Rice," she said. "And then," she said, louder, "the postal worker. Undercovers picked him up while he was doing his job because he looked at them funny. He was in his uniform, with his mail truck. He was in the same training class as my husband. Could have been my husband." Dr. Harris leaned over the kitchen island like it was her podium and Nikki was her jury. "If this country were my patient, I'd say it was beyond help. Nothing I can do to save it. But I can save my kids." She pointed a slim finger at Nikki. "I can leave."

On the couch, Derrick smiled and rubbed his nose in a way that reminded Nikki of Marcus. She remembered the night they were coming home from a concert in Prospect Park and a cop stopped them. Later, Marcus made light of it, saying it was the last time he'd ever wear cargo shorts because there were so many pockets for the cop to search. But that night, his hands shook so violently that he couldn't unzip his jacket.

Dr. Harris had resumed her chopping again. Maybe she has the right idea, Nikki thought. Maybe we should all head north. In her mind, she could picture it, hundreds of thousands of black people driving across the Canadian boarder, welcomed by smiling Canucks carrying cases of Molson's and boxes of Tim Hortons doughnuts. Justin Trudeau would hug everyone personally and teach them the Canadian national anthem.

"Where's your computer?" Nikki asked. "And the documents you've already put together. Even if you're planning to leave, we've got to submit it. We'll do it together."

A few hours later, they'd finalized the Harris family's paperwork for homeschooling. And when Nikki reported on the case in her case review that was supposed to be weekly but always ended up being monthly, Nikki gave her supervisor copies of everything. Nikki told her that Dr. Harris had been homeschooling since September and following a well-established IHIP, but her paperwork had been lost by the DOE. Because no one doubts the DOE's ability to lose paperwork. And that was that.

*   *   *

It was spring before Nikki was on New York Avenue again, on her way to another home visit (corporal punishment—gruesome). It was that first real day of spring when the sun gets aggressive, yanking tulips from the ground, their leaves reaching from the dirt like hands. As Nikki approached the Harris place, she thought of the pile of graduate school applications on the milk crate next to her futon. McGill. LSE. Toronto. Nikki had told her grandma at Christmas. They'd been in the living room, sipping hot toddies next to the plastic tree that they put together every year.

As Nikki talked, her grandma took off her glasses and rubbed them with a handkerchief. When she put them back on, they magnified her tears. Her mouth set in a tight smile, she held out her arms for a hug.

"Guess I'll finally have to go down to the post office and get a passport," she said, rubbing Nikki's back. "But I'm not letting that troglodyte at the counter take my picture; security will think I'm a terrorist. I'm getting my photo done at the Walgreens."

At the Harris place, there was a Corcoran sign in the yard with a glossy red SOLD sticker, just like on HGTV. This time, Charisse was on the stoop next door. Or there was a woman who Nikki imagined to be Charisse, drinking coffee and smoking a cigarette.

Nikki stopped at the wrought-iron gate and looked up at the windows, which were slightly open, each one with a new home-security decal in the shape of a stop sign. The Harris's shades were gone, replaced by white curtains that shifted slightly in the breeze, like lazy ghosts.

"Canada," the woman on the stoop said when she noticed Nikki. "The grandmother had been in that place since the fifties, and the granddaughter sold it to some Australian banker. Up and went to Canada." She shook her head while she ashed her cigarette. "Not going to be any black people left in Brooklyn soon."

Nikki stood with one hand on the gate, still cool from the morning chill. She looked up, and a triangle of geese winged its way across the sky. As she watched them, she wondered whether the geese ever got angry when their instincts forced them to leave a perfectly nice lake and fly far away.

————————

MICHELE HOST *is a lawyer and writer living in Brooklyn. Her fiction has been published in The Prick of the Spindle, and her nonfiction has been published in The Huffington Post.*

Speakers of Other Languages
Maria Thomas

O swald thought of mulch as he took a seat outside the Botanic
Gardens. The word was satisfying and he said it aloud, to
a pair of closed iron gates: "mulch." He said it again, and then
a couple more times, and then lots: "Mulch, mulch, mulch."
Nobody was around to hear him. The wide suburban street was
quiet except for a dog crying from inside a house, and there
were no signs of life, human life at least, inside the Botanic
Gardens. The place shut early on Friday afternoons but Oswald
had stepped off the bus there anyway because he couldn't quite
face going home. "The main point of mulch," he said, again to
nobody, "is to make everything just right." Then he wondered
if he hadn't finally gone a bit mad.

An hour earlier, Oswald had lost his job of forty-two years.
He was sixty-three. Three years older than his wife, who was
always waiting at home for him irritated, and three years younger than his father had been when he died, was cremated, and
then scattered over his own glorious garden in another English
market town. Oswald felt giddy. Maths and mulch, that was life
boiled down. He bowed his head and began counting slowly,
touching the cracked tips of his fingers, trying to arrange his
numbers in their proper order. In all things, order offered meaning, and meaning offered solace. Somewhere around thirty he
felt steadier. A heavy shower at lunchtime had lifted the smell
of soil and the sweet decay of the Gardens' flora into the air; it

was pleasant and Oswald remembered he was grateful for the commitment of lifetime membership, for his place amid the quiet rot.

Which was just as well because he had no place else to be, now that Hannity Textiles had deemed travelling sales primitive and Oswald too slow, too analog for anything different. Apparently he was too domestic, also. Mr. Dole had said things about the company changing, about moving whole divisions abroad, giving the poor, blighted people in the third world something to do. He had called this *outsourcing*. Over and over he'd said it: *outsourcing*. As if repetition would help this phrase make sense.

Oswald stood and peered through the iron gates, past a large Photinia fraseri. He was disappointed to find nobody with hands in the dirt, nobody at work. What made Fridays different than any other day people were supposed to be doing their jobs? The Wednesday before, deep inside the Botanic Gardens, he had spotted a group of laborers removing glass from a dilapidated hothouse. It had calmed him, watching the strong young men move behind their hazard barrier, studying how they punched out glass with gloved fists and tossed the shards into wheelbarrows in fluid motions, with no fear they might miss. The whole thing might've been a ballet. They'd been silent except for the occasional instruction in a musical, robust language Oswald had suspected was Polish. It seemed a long time ago.

In fact, everything did. In particular, Oswald's youth, which felt to him now like something of a foreign concept, or an affliction that had affected a distant relative. Various dinner companions and members of his wife's circle were always talking about how they "still felt like teenagers on the inside," but this was not a sensation he shared, and nor was it one whose absence he had lamented. Until, perhaps, watching the Polish dancers.

Oswald grabbed the locked gates of the Botanic Gardens and gave them a shake so brisk he felt the iron resist in his bones. His wife Audie had many plans for his retirement. She'd scheduled a South of France river cruise, a course in antiques appraisal, and wine tasting weekends with their neighbors, the Johnsons. She'd been enthusiastic about the prospect of having Oswald around so he could help with her DIY *adventures*, and so they could lunch on coquilles St.-Jacques together at the new brasserie in town. She'd determined their existence empty and demanded it filled. Oswald rattled the gates once again.

*   *   *

Audie removed Ron Rossiter's hand from her knee and rose from the table to dump an extra serving of boeuf bourguignon onto Oswald's plate. Some of the gravy splashed on his favorite tie and she felt a little pleased, given he'd come home so late and left her to deal with cocktail hour, the Johnsons, Ron Rossiter, and his new, idiot wife, alone.

"So, what held you up, Oswald?"

"In general?" Ted Johnson said with a snort.

"Tonight," Audie sniped, but her husband's attention was lost, to beef that melted in the mouth. Deflated, Audie dropped onto her chair.

"You'd think they'd let him out early on a Friday," Janice Rossiter said, shaking her great dyed dolly-bird head. "Poor old Oswald. No afternoon delight." She winked at her husband who was stuffing hunks of homemade fougasse into his mouth, and reached across the table for his hand. Audie cringed.

"Tough times over there, I hear." Ted Johnson dabbed his lips with a napkin. "You know Hannity Linens let our Jenny go?"

"She never showed up to work, Ted," Sue Johnson snapped. She smiled at everyone else apologetically. "Jenny's bone idle. But then you've got that Polish girl—Anna I think her name is—who runs herself ragged in that shop. I don't know what'll happen when they all get kicked out, honestly I don't."

"Who?" Audie asked.

"The Polish. All the Europeans."

"We don't know they're going, yet," Ron Rossiter offered.

"Well they should. Good riddance," Ted Johnson said. "Send 'em all back to where they came from and quick sharpish. My Jenny almost never got that job because of those Polish girls. Had to fight for it, she did."

"Fight for it?" Sue Johnson set her jaw and spoke through her teeth. "Oswald made a bloody phone call. And she didn't exactly fight to keep the job did she, Ted? It's no bloody wonder she got fired."

"I didn't get fired," Oswald said, suddenly looking up from his plate.

Audie stared at him. "Nobody's saying you did."

"I was made redundant."

"When?"

"This afternoon."

There was silence. Audie could sense her guests' anticipation but she studied her husband's face carefully. A deep furrow in his forehead mirrored the cleft in his chin that she'd once thought quite sexy; a nerve jumped at one corner of his thin, frowning mouth. He'd aged so quickly it seemed, although, perhaps not. It had been years since she'd really looked at him. "Good," she said.

"What?"

"I said good. Let's celebrate. That fool Kenny Dole can run the place himself."

"Chin, chin!" Ron Rossiter mumbled with a mouth full of bread, and they all raised their glasses to Oswald, who responded with an embarrassed nod.

"What will you do now?" Sue Johnson asked after taking a large gulp of wine.

"I'd invest," her husband said. "Build a little nest egg for my Jenny."

Sue sighed and reached for the carafe. "Audie, do you still want that extension? Our Marlene got one on her redundancy. We can put you in touch with her builders." She narrowed her eyes at her husband and poured herself another glass. "They're Polish."

Oswald rose and began to clear the empty plates. Audie watched his slow, deliberate movements with growing frustration. "We'll see. I'd like to travel, maybe live abroad. I'm sick to death of it here."

"That-a girl!" Ron Rossiter said, and drained the last of his wine. Oswald disappeared into the kitchen without a word.

*   *   *

Later that night, Audie sat up in bed and read over the information

Ken Dole had given Oswald. His pension was safe and the redundancy settlement was appropriately large, but Audie didn't expect her husband to be happy about it. He hated change. Hated the switch from butter to margarine because of his cholesterol, the new wallpaper in the living room, every hairdo she'd gotten since 1970 and, admittedly to his credit, every new-fangled wife Ron Rossiter had ever had. It didn't matter, Audie thought. The money was a chance, a precious, long-awaited opportunity.

"Oswald," she called as he shuffled past on the way to his bedroom. He reappeared in the doorway.

"Everything okay?"

"It's better than that. Look."

Oswald perched on the edge of her bed. She showed him the figures and he nodded like Ron Rossiter's absurd dashboard dog. "Don't you see?" Audie said. "Maybe we could get a little place abroad? France, perhaps?" She placed a hand on his arm and he moved, just slightly, away from her.

"I don't think so, Audie."

"All this Brexit business won't stop us buying over there, surely."

"It's not that."

"So what is it? There's nothing keeping us here. Nobody. Why don't we try something new? It doesn't have to be France. We can go anywhere you like. We could—"

"This is our home." Oswald straightened up then stood. His height made him seem even more stubborn, and it maddened her that after all their years of marriage she still found this attractive.

"Well," she yelled at his back, feeling childish even as the words formed. "If I'm going to be stuck in *our home*, I'm going to make this fucking house a whole lot bigger!"

*   *   *

Audie watched through the kitchen window as Oswald pruned a giant shrub rose. She wished the sink were in another position so she didn't have to look out into his precious garden every time she did the washing up. The main problem was that she couldn't deny what he'd created was utterly beautiful, the envy, in fact, of their small market town. In spring and summer

Audie would often answer the front door to complete strangers who'd heard about her husband's efforts. Some days she'd direct them to the back gate and let them through to nose about; other days she would refuse to play along and close the door on them, firmly but without malice, just as she did with the local Jehovah's Witnesses.

Those enthusiasts lucky enough to be granted entry usually wanted to praise her if Oswald was at work. They screeched over how wild the garden was: honeysuckle seducing whole fences; roses claiming the entire west face of Oswald's potting shed; the trumpet vine and clematis hugging the walls of their house, blooms angling upward, toward the light.

Or these strangers would come prepared with crisp handkerchiefs and comment on how fragrant it was: *such a joy for the birds and the bees!* Pushing their noses into the bridal wreath, running their cupped palms gently up shafts of lavender to explore the scent on their own bodies.

Occasionally there were those who came only to see the kitchen garden. They would take polite notice of the gladioli and cornflowers, but before the courgette blooms and carrot tops they would beam and stroke their chins and say things like "bountiful," "marvelous," and "he must put his heart and soul into this. *His heart and soul.*"

Audie routinely found herself exhausted.

Outside, Oswald moved to the bench and cradled a potted plant in his lap, wiping its leaves with a chamois. He'd always loved horticulture—he'd been that way when Audie met him and it had actually been one of the things she'd liked: how sensitive he was, how he spoke about plants as if they were miracles, how he'd conversed with her in almost the same way, respectfully, deferentially, something that despite everything had never changed. The week they bought the house, he'd immediately set to work, clearing scrub, pulling up weeds and disposing of odd bits of rubble. As the years went by he retreated into the space further and further, until his presence in the house came as a surprise to Audie. On those rare occasions that she caught him in an armchair, watching television or reading *The Telegraph*, her presence—a mere attempt to engage him on a subject as benign as the weather—would be enough to send him fleeing to his Eden once again.

Audie grew to hate the garden. She had dreams about it burning, sending huge flames into a dark night sky. After the last Hannity Christmas party, she had come home alive with anger and the effects of cheap house wine, and taken a pair of shears to his precious wisteria. She'd hacked at the plant, while Oswald stood in the gloom and watched. He didn't ask why, didn't try to stop her, and he never mentioned it again. This impotence came as no surprise.

Now, Audie slowly scrubbed the inside of a novelty Sacré Coeur teapot, working the dish brush into its crevices. Oswald was in his throes of passion, completely engrossed, now, in planting bulbs for spring. She wanted to see if he would stop her building the extension.

The planning permission had come through quickly; the call was in to Sue Johnson's Polish builders—they would be round to measure up in a few days. Oswald had been unsettled, disturbed, even, in the weeks since leaving Hannity. This was the time to move forward. If not now then never. She wondered how far she could push him before he would crack.

Of course, the affairs hadn't made a bit of difference and Audie was sure Oswald had known. She hadn't tried to hide it. *Au contraire*. The first dalliance, when she'd been married only a year, was with a man named Geoffrey who worked in the bakery directly opposite Hannity Linens on the high street. She'd accepted his under-baked scones and loaves and fed them to Oswald who, after only a few months or so of trying, had decided that sex with his wife was not at all for him. Audie had never really thought sex was much for her, either, and being from a large unwieldy family, children had never mattered awfully, but this wasn't right. She was no authority on marital relations, but she knew this wasn't the way things were supposed to go, and worse, his disinterest seemed to confirm her deepest fears. On her wedding day, Audie's sister Peggy had cruelly joked that she'd long suspected Oswald was of the "other way." What the bloody hell kind of curse was that on a girl giddy in love?

The next two, or three, men had been colleagues of his at Hannity Textiles, and that had been deliberate. Audie had made a shamefully easy play for Mr. Hannity himself, extending an invitation to visit the garden he'd been dying to see, while Oswald was on the road, pretending to sell the old man's shitty linens to cheap hotels. It made her shudder to think of Hannity's decrepit flesh, probably not entirely unlike her own now, too soft and bulbous, easier than ever to bruise.

There were others over the decades but then, finally, ten years ago: Ron Rossiter. The crown prince of import-export, a man she didn't even like, much less find attractive. It lasted a week. One night, when Oswald was on an extended trip in Scotland, Ron had come over looking for some excuse to talk to her and she'd caved. It may've been the talk of France, his pidgin French, his knowledge of wines and the exotic kinds of people he met in his line of work. It may not have been any of those things but France was what stuck, and Audie had clung to it ever since, like Janice Rossiter clung to an idea of youth and Sue Johnson clung to Marks and Spencer's Merlot.

Ron Rossiter took Audie on a trip to Calais. They ate in a restaurant that served bouillabaisse she was sure had been prepared using tinned tuna, and later that night in a Holiday Inn they had sex for the final time. It was awkward and they both smelled faintly of garlic and tomato concentrate; they executed the kind of grubby, half-hearted coupling that makes people desperate for a long shower, alone. While Ron took one, Audie crossed her arms over her large, flat breasts and wondered if, by some biological miracle, he had made her pregnant. It needn't be dramatic, she thought. The menopause could wait another year or so. She could go to mother and baby coffee mornings and luncheons, and learn how to speak French so she could teach the baby when it got old enough and eventually they would have conversations that sounded passionate and spirited.

Bébé. Maman. Joie de vivre.

It seemed to be a condition of the new century that people who didn't know they wanted things suddenly wanted them because they happened, and that was life. Sue Johnson's elder sister became a Hare Krishna in 2000 because her yoga teacher boyfriend was. Then she had what Sue called a "real awakening." The couple moved to India, and as far as anyone knew or cared, they were happy. Maybe having a baby by Ron Rossister at age fifty was as simple as signing up for yoga.

The suds in the sink had disappeared and Audie realized her hands were cold. She dried them on an Eiffel towel and took a last look at Oswald in his garden, smiling at a hydrangea, content. He'd never had an affair of his own, she knew that much. Not unless you counted the foliage. His crush on that insufferable Kenny Dole had driven her to distraction at the last Hannity Christmas party, but it wasn't the fact of it so much as its insipid quality, the absolute impossibility of it, Kenny Dole being oblivious and straight as a die, and Oswald demure as a forties housewife anytime the object of his lust came within spitting distance. Really, was it a wife's job to point out such a thing to her husband?

Enough is enough, Audie thought, pulling the Sacré Coeur teapot from the sink and tossing it into the kitchen bin. Let the Polish build the damn extension. If they make it to the roof, I'm gone.

*   *   *

When Oswald returned from a morning browsing seedlings at the Botanic Gardens, the builders had already marked out the rectangular boundary of the extension with pegs and string.

"You haven't pulled anything up," Audie said, and flicked the bell of a foxglove. "So, I let the builders have a long lunch. They'll be back in an hour or so. You can clear this by then, right?" She handed Oswald a shovel and went inside.

The part of the garden in the extension space was among Oswald's favorites. He loved the climbers and trailers that covered the wall of the house, enjoyed watching their sly progress under eaves, around corners, and across the crumbling Victorian brick. He stared at the expanse of green tangle and red, white, and purple flowers on the wall, the rash of poppies and lupine at its feet, then laid the shovel on the path and stepped over the string marker. Once inside it, the space was bigger than he thought, but then wasn't that always the case with building projects? Audie had shown him the plans, even run through them with him, marking out the extension with bright yellow duct tape and pointing to each plant that would have to go and which ones near the boundary that should probably be pulled too, but he hadn't registered any of it and now, on the precipice of eviction from his own little corner of paradise, he felt helpless, bereft.

Oswald knelt down and as the damp seeped through his corduroys, he began to tug at the roots around him. He pulled and grabbed and tore at foliage, picking up speed as he went, tossing prickly handfuls then great armfuls over the string boundary, his whole body turned mechanical, consumed by the task of clearing the rectangle. He was in such a trance he didn't notice Audie looming over him.

"Oswald," she said. "Oswald. Stop. Please."

He looked up, panting. Her plump face was wan and clammy like she'd been crying but he didn't care to ask why. He had been feeling a lot, in the weeks since leaving Hannity, like he could not bring himself to care a fig about anything. "But I'm nearly finished," he said.

"The builders will do the rest," she said, shaking her head. "They'll be back soon. Here." She threw a flannel at him and he wiped the sweat and dirt from his face.

"I'm almost done. I'll get a ladder and—"

"Just leave it will you, Oswald, for Christ's sake," Audie shouted. "It's what we're bloody paying them for isn't it?"

"Problems?" A fat, bearded man with a bag of cement slung over one shoulder was at the back gate. Two younger men, partially obscured, flanked him. "Not interrupting are we?"

"No, no, Jimmy. Come on in. Get started," Audie said, gesturing at the almost bald rectangle of garden before her. "My husband's done the best he could."

Oswald heard the false cheer in her voice but Jimmy advanced, grinning. Men liked Audie. She was a plain, broad woman, but they sensed she was warm and comforting, just like Oswald had, once his mother had convinced him to meet her. "Audie Mills," the old woman had said, "is a sound option. She'll do right by you, if you do right by her."

The taller of the younger men pulled a small yellow cement mixer behind him on a length of rope and the other carried a hod. Oswald eyed them carefully. They were sullen but clearly capable, and they set about removing the remainder of foliage from the rectangle while their boss made small talk with Audie about disruptions, timescales and finishes; of course they would have to knock out most of her precious kitchen wall. The shorter man was most graceful, despite his stout frame. He stooped and swung his torso low to the ground, scooping and scraping debris from the dirt. It occurred to Oswald that he might've been one of the men who labored at the Botanic Gardens, one of the dancers. It made him smile.

"Oswald," Audie cawed in such a way he suddenly felt inexplicably guilty. "Leave the poor fellows to their work."

The shorter man turned to look at him, as though he realized he was the one being watched. His eyes, set deep in his tanned, square face, were an opaque blue, and a small scar on his lip made it look as though he was snarling. Oswald wanted to kiss it.

*   *   *

The men worked quickly and within a week plastic sheeting covered the gaping hole in the house, foundations had been laid, and the extension walls were a foot high. Oswald spent his time in his potting shed, thinning seedlings and watching the man with the snarl through a cracked window he'd cleaned thoroughly, so as to get a better view. It was the thing he looked forward to most and he began to make a study of the man, first arbitrarily assigning moods to his clothes (jeans, happy; dungarees, depressed), then to his mannerisms (lip touch, pensive; neck roll, tense), and then, Oswald assigned him histories, fully imagined pasts, silly, romantic trajectories toward this point in time, the point of their meeting.

The one Oswald played most often was how the man got his snarl: as a teenager he'd dared defy his overbearing father by refusing to marry a local girl, and the father, enraged, had struck him across the face with a vodka bottle. *Pow!* Determined to live his own life, he'd fled to Warsaw, then England, and had made his way across the country working in beautiful gardens ever since. It pleased and stirred Oswald to think an act of defiance had brought the man into his Eden.

After a week, when the door and window frames were in and the walls were nearing five feet tall, Oswald believed he knew everything there was to know about the man with the snarl. Then, when he was searching for plant labels, the man knocked on his shed door.

"Your wife, she's gone to shops. We can use facility?" His English was better than Oswald had expected; his voice was deep but mellow, kind somehow.

"Facility?"

"Toilet."

"Yes. Yes, of course! Please, go on in!"

The exchange left Oswald desperate. When Audie returned from the supermarket and circled around the men with cups of tea on a tray, he emerged from his shed and strolled over to them, as nonchalantly as he could.

"Everything okay over here?" Oswald asked, feeling the nerve in his lip come alive.

"This is my husband, Oswald," Audie said to the men. "Oswald, this is Jimmy. He's the foreman. This is Bartek, and this is Casimir."

Casimir. It was truly wonderful when people belonged to their names.

"Hello." Oswald extended his hand to the man with the snarl who looked at it quizzically for a second. He shook it, and Oswald realized he was missing most of his ring finger. He had a stub that twitched gently against Oswald's palm, a rough, incomplete handshake that was entirely perfect.

Audie took a step back and stared at the reclaimed brick of the extension wall. The other two men were doubtless looking at her husband looking at Casimir, but she found it hard to. She hadn't expected to feel jealousy, but there it was, certain and bold as Oswald's attraction to the short Polish builder. She tried to focus on being surprised, on how Oswald had pushed his way into this circle of men and staked a claim on one of them, in front of her no less. It was out of character, and though slighted, she had to admit his behavior was impressive.

Maybe it signified something. Maybe it meant he would leave her soon, just pack up his shrubs and go. It had only taken a moment but she could read his shifts like a seismograph and now it seemed like such a thing could happen. And wasn't it what she had wanted, the whole point of trashing his beloved sanctuary? Would it actually be so damn dreadful, so scandalous?

It was the new millennium after all, and somewhere along the line it had been decided that it was now fine for anyone to do whatever the hell they pleased. Divorce was *de rigueur*. Being the former wife of a gay pensioner was slightly more exotic, but hardly revolutionary, either. Audie felt twisted inside. The men went back to their work and Oswald wandered back to his shed.

*   *   *

The following week, Jimmy disappeared to oversee another job and Oswald spent Monday morning sipping coffee and trying to make idle conversation with Bartek and Casimir. To Oswald's disappointment but not to his surprise, Bartek was the chattier of the two, and told him all about his English wife—born in Sheffield—and baby on the way, his home in Gdynia, and his grief with some local Lithuanians. He spoke at length about pulling the trigger on Article 50. Oswald nodded and smiled and kept watch on Casimir who only seemed interested in mortar until Bartek asked Oswald what team he supported.

"Oh, football you mean?"

"Yes, your team?" Casimir stepped down from his ladder and took a pull from a can of Irn-Bru. The walls were now around six feet.

"Well, I . . . " Oswald fumbled for a side, a good one, a team that had won something. Casimir was staring at him and Oswald's mouth began to twitch again. "I—"

"Manchester United?" Bartek offered, hopefully.

"No. Chelsea," said Casimir matter-of-factly.

Oswald blushed at the gesture. It *was* a gesture. Casimir had claimed him. "Yes, Chelsea. Great team."

Casimir frowned for a moment, but he then proceeded to talk about his passion for the London side. He recalled a visit to their stadium at Stamford Bridge, a memory that made him smile, the first Oswald had seen on Casimir's mangled lip since he had arrived. It was a blissful ten minutes, and Audie, who Oswald sensed had her eye on them all from the kitchen window, didn't interrupt once.

Around noon, a young woman appeared at the back gate. She was tall and fine-boned, with dirty blonde hair pulled up into a chignon on top of her head. Oswald spotted her through the potting shed window and, as she gingerly stepped into his garden, he realized she looked vaguely familiar. She cantered toward the extension and, for a moment, Oswald thought she must be Bartek's wife, but when he opened his shed door and stepped out to see, it was clear there wasn't a speck of Sheffield about her. It was Anna, the Polish girl from the Hannity shop on the high street, and she wasn't in his garden to visit Bartek; she had come for Casimir.

He jumped off the ladder when he saw her and pulled her into his chest with one great arm, relieving her of a plastic Sainsbury's bag with the other. That's his lunch, Oswald thought, and the idea of her in the supermarket taking time to choose Casimir's sandwich, or worse, at home in their kitchen, buttering his bread, made him unsteady with rage. Casimir kissed her on the cheek and honked her chignon like it was a clown's nose, a playful gesture that seemed so unlike him and suggested the pair were friends as well as lovers. Oswald wanted to advance, to exterminate her like the pest she was, but he couldn't move, he could only watch them flirting shamelessly, in his garden that he had made paradise, as though he didn't exist.

On cue, Audie came outside with a tray of teacups. She's been spying too, thought Oswald, and it occurred to him that maybe she also thought Casimir was attractive, and wanted his attention. She couldn't have it. She could have the extension; that was hers. But she couldn't have Casimir, and neither, it seemed, could he. His wife shook hands with Anna and they talked, the girl smiling and Audie large and animated, but Oswald couldn't make out what they were saying until Audie screeched, "why, that's lovely news! Come on, Anna, I've got something to show you." The two women disappeared inside and Casimir watched them go, his broad, sweat-stained back to Oswald like a drawn curtain.

*   *   *

Audie led Anna upstairs to her bedroom. They had met before, a couple of times, and Anna had been polite, efficient, happy to give Audie more of a discount in Hannity Linens than she was really entitled. Audie liked the girl and thought she saw in her a depth that she sometimes spotted in people from tortured places. She wanted to ask Anna questions—about Poland, about Casimir, about sex and being twenty-something, about having it all to look forward to—but when Audie offered her a seat on the bed Anna's coy expression prevented it. She was just a girl.

"So, he can't afford a ring, yet?" Audie seated herself on her vanity stool.

"No. He's trying. He says soon. Very soon."

Audie smiled at this. "Well, that won't do, will it?" She rifled through the jewelry box on the vanity, and pulled from it a pair of diamond drop earrings Oswald had once bought her. "I knew they were in here somewhere!"

Anna's mossy eyes widened as Audie held them out. "Take these," Audie said. "They're real. Casimir will get a good price for them."

"No, we couldn't. It is kind, but they are too much." Anna blushed and dipped her head, shyly.

"Go on, take them. I want you to have them."

"Why?" Anna said, looking up.

"Just because. I think you should have them. I think he should pawn them and buy you a ring. A big sparkler. The biggest he can get. I think you should have whatever it is you want and be happy."

Audie laughed and the girl laughed too. She was beautiful. Audie placed the diamonds gently in her hand and clasped it shut.

"But what about your children? If you don't want the earrings, you should give them to your children."

Audie shook her head. "We don't have any, dear."

"I'm sorry," Anna said softly, and placed a white, slender hand on Audie's. The idea of a life without children probably horrified her. There are worse things, thought Audie, and she wished she could tell them, but it wouldn't sound right.

"Can I ask, why?"

"We just didn't get around to it."

"I see," Anna said, but it was obvious she didn't. "That is hard."

"Aha! That, my girl," Audie said, patting Anna's hand, "is life." And despite this being a sad sort of truth, it sounded as false as it felt.

*   *   *

Oswald wanted to get closer and he made his way to the extension just as Anna was leaving the house. Audie came out with her.

"Oswald, this is Anna. She's Casimir's fiancé."

Anna held out her hand but Oswald couldn't take it. He didn't mean to be rude, but he couldn't make himself do it. The girl glanced at Audie and nervously touched her ear; she was wearing Audie's diamond earrings. Ones he had bought Audie with every last penny he had so many years ago. He stared at his wife, who stared right back.

"What is this?" Oswald said, feeling his face grow warm, hearing an unfamiliar growl creep into his own voice.

"Oh, the earrings? Yes, I gave them to Anna and Casimir. They need a bit of help. So they can get married and live happily ever after, even after this stupid country sends them home. I haven't worn the old things in twenty years. What are they to me?" Audie turned and laughed at Anna, who was staring up at Casimir on the ladder.

"I have to go back to work, now," the girl said. "Thank you, Audie. Thank you, Oswald." She waved goodbye to Casimir and Bartek and left, taking even quicker steps this time, out of the garden.

Clouds passed over the sky and the two men, who were almost ready to add the roof to the extension, looked ridiculous, like clowns balancing on toy ladders. Oswald and Audie faced each other and—an impulse completely and surprisingly new to him—Oswald wanted to place his hands around his wife's neck and choke every ounce of life from her. It took all his strength to stop himself from actually doing it. "I gave you those diamonds," he said.

Audie didn't reply. She just stared at him, her mouth set in a strange crooked way. Oswald couldn't look at her. Shaking, he turned and made his way back to the shed.

*   *   *

That night, Audie woke to a loud crashing sound outside. She slid out of bed, chilly in only a chemise, and pulled back her curtain. The moon was big and bright and below, in its sheen, Oswald was smashing the walls of the extension with a sledge-hammer, putting the whole weight of his body into each deliberate, devastating swing. Audie watched him for a while, her bare feet growing numb with cold. Her husband was magnificent and she willed him on until he had decimated almost half the structure. She remembered the day he'd given her the earrings. The sun had shone on a trip to the Botanic Gardens, and they'd walked hand in hand along the serpentine paths, pausing so that they both could admire the exhibits. Oswald had explained them and Audie had listened. On a bench, over a cheese and pickle sandwich, he'd held open a plush red box and inside had been, in that moment at least, everything a plain and overlooked girl needed to feel pretty. He'd been so proud of himself, and of her. He'd kissed her shyly on the cheek and touched the diamonds in her ears, and she'd known he was a good choice, that he would care.

In his way, he had. But now the earrings belonged to someone else.

Oswald took one great swing at a corner that tumbled the last of the ugly structure. He looked up and Audie saw that his face was terrible: a tragic mask. All she needed was a single deep breath, a numb footstep in any direction. She moved from the window and dragged a suitcase from the top of her wardrobe. She blew and swept the dust from it, flipped it open, and slowly began to pack her things.

MARIA THOMAS gained her MFA from the University of Oregon. She is currently a PhD candidate in Creative Writing at Goldsmiths, University of London, where she is at work on a novel about female sex tourism in the Caribbean. Her recent fiction has appeared in Wasafiri: International and Contemporary Writing. She lives in London, with her books.

Steal Away

Nicole Cuffy

The planting season was just around the corner, and then the cotton would grow right up to the door of their shack. They'd chop it down, make it full, and then picking season: fingertips cured to leather, toneless sounding of the old plantation bell, aching feet busting out of shoes, hot sun like a whip through the clothes on your back.

The work was slave work. From see to don't see, first light to blackest dark. The drought had made them desperate; the harvest was poor. And now their debt was even deeper. Slavery. Ida, shortly after Irving was born, had offered to pull them out, to pay the debt to Mr. Lysee and set them up in the North. But Hester, angry that it had taken so long for Ida to offer, and angry that it was an offer she needed to make, had refused to accept anything from her sister. She burned the letter so Reggie would never know what she'd turned down. And indeed, the offer was never made again.

Ida, the beautiful, yellow, older sister who'd found everything their parents had wanted her to find up North, everything their father had shucked and jived into giving her until it killed him. And Hester, dark Hester, stuck in the dark South, face smooth as a myrtle leaf, hands as rough as the bark. It had been six months since Ida's husband had died, and Hester had not heard from her sister since then. She worried for her—always so small, so fragile. Over the years, Hester had learned to love her sister despite what their parents, the North, the South, separation and time had done to them. Though, that wasn't quite the thing—she had always loved her sister, had always admired her. But that love, for many years, had been trapped, stubbornly breathing, underneath a great hurt.

Hester stood to her full height, something in her back cracking as she did. The drought had left Irving and Reggie skinnier, and her dry in her bones, so that now, she cracked and popped like fall twigs when she stretched. She'd planted her little vegetable garden early this year, praying it would grow. Sweet potatoes, string beans, collard greens, turnips, cabbage, and onions. In a couple of months when the ground warmed up, she'd plant the lima beans, the black-eyed peas, and the tomatoes, too. Last year, only the onions and peas had grown, and only sparsely at that. They'd eaten a pot of black-eyed peas and rice for nearly the whole year.

Buttermilk was running around through the turned dirt, barking at nothing. Hester sucked her teeth and shooed her away. Yaller, the cat, watched the scene impassively from the branches of a fat, sour apple tree. Buttoning up her coat, Hester went inside, where the hominy porridge was simmering on top of the wood burning stove, the fried chicken livers and biscuits already on the table. It was almost noontime, and Reggie would be coming in from the field any minute for dinner. She set the hominy on a cloth on the table, and set a pot of beef broth, cabbage, and kidney beans on the stove in its place to simmer—it would be their supper later.

Reggie came in with Sylvester and Tirzah, their neighbors, and their five children—Tobiah, Rissa, Abraham, Jacob, and Damaris. During the planting and picking seasons, Hester, Reggie, and their neighbors took turns helping each other with the plowing, hoeing, planting, cutting, and picking. Hester and Reggie especially needed the help because, unlike all of their neighbors, they only had one child. A crueler landlord would have kicked them out long ago for being a no-account family. But Mr. Lysee had known Hester her whole life, and her family had served his for generations—Hester's grandparents had been slaves on this land.

And for a white landlord, he was not a bad man—though the crops spanned many acres and the cotton grew to their door, they had a stove, a good, deep well, and a sturdy outhouse, and that was more than could be said for some of their neighbors. Some of their neighbors moved from plantation to plantation, always working on halves. But the Lysee plantation was their home, and they didn't move without Lysee's permission. And Lysee would only give his permission if some other rich planter decided to take over the debt. This was how Lysee ran his business, just like his father and grandfather before him. He considered Hester's family loyal, and because he considered them loyal, he treated them as well as was proper for a white man to treat colored people.

The roof in the kitchen leaked. On rainy days, Hester set out a tin pail to catch the water, which she saved in a barrel in the storehouse in case they got a dry spell, or their well got low. And on cold winter days, she stuffed the leak with raw cotton. The source of the leak was a small hole in the roof, which, on warm summer days, blared either white or blue, depending on the position of the sun. On the days when the roof leaked, Reggie grumbled about meaning to fix it, but come good weather, he always forgot. And Hester never reminded him.

The truth of it was that Hester loved that hole in the roof almost religiously. In the mornings, in that brief, sacred time when she was the only one awake in the house except for Yaller, before she began to fix breakfast, she always spared a moment to peek through the hole—in the winter, she took out the wad of cotton to do this—and the swatch of winter slate or summer heather sky she glimpsed was to her as godly as black Word typeset onto Bible pages. By the time she stepped outside to begin her day's work, that winter slate or summer heather had already shifted into something else, the sky morphing as the sun opened its mouth over the country.

This country, Mississippi country, to those who did not pay enough attention to its small miracles, was rough, rusty, and flat, and covered all over with a persistent dusting of silence. But Hester, who always tried to pay close attention to God and His forms, saw it for what it really was: red, dropsical, fat with life.

There was Hester and her family, the other halvers, the white tenant farmers, the small farmers who lived near the highway front, the merchants and shopkeeps, the policemen and doctors and veterinarians and lawyers, the judge and the mayor, and presiding over them all, the royal families, the wealthy planters, the landlords, who ruled their own hierarchical courts—plantation-manager, overseer, riding boss, sharecropper.

But the life in this country was even bigger than that. There were the field mice, the rats, the rabbits, the squirrels, the red foxes, the possum, the nutria, the skunks, the coyotes, who were often only a rumor. Then white-tailed deer, spiders, bats, rattlers, cottonmouths, copperheads, milksnakes who sucked at the cows' teats if you didn't watch for them around the barn. Ground frogs and tree frogs, ragged razorbacks, shining black flies, bloated fever mosquitoes and tiny, undiseased mosquitoes.

Aside from the animals Hester didn't tend, were the ones she did—the hens, who, come spring, Hester mated to the neighbor's rooster; the scarred mules, their dark eyes wet and sleepy; the red hogs kept fat with corn cobs, sweet potatoes, and manna; the dull, spoke-hipped cows with their grayish udders. There were two dogs. One—a doe-eyed mutt named Salt and Pepper after the pattern of his fur—belonged to Reggie, and was decent enough at catching cottontails that Reggie frequently took him along to hunt. Hoyt Morrison, a white shopkeep, gave that dog to Reggie years ago. The second dog, Buttermilk, belonged to no one.

To Hester, this country, stretched thin over red dirt but lousy with living, was God's Word just as surely as the scripture was, and so all of its life was holy. Even Mr. Boll Weevil. Even Yaller, who left bloody thrush carcasses on the porch but never bothered with rats or mice. Negroes understood this. Hester had heard that Indians understood it too. But sometimes she'd see white folks beating at mules who wouldn't mind, dogs who got too rowdy, and the black folks around would quietly shake their heads. The way was to talk, to understand.

But some white folks had something in them that made them hate something that was its own thing, something that could never truly be owned. There were some black folks that way too. But the way Hester saw it, white or black, people were

God's Word too, this country God's country, and that hole in the roof, through which she studied the slate or the heather each morning, was her prayer.

Irving fell asleep early, exhausted after a day spent helping to terrace the rice field. The rice was not a staple crop or a cash crop—their staple was corn and their cash was cotton, but ever since the great flood of '27 had missed them by only ten miles, Mr. Lysee insisted on having a crop, besides the peanuts, that could withstand the water. In the drought last year, the crop had failed. But he had insisted on it again this year, and he'd had an expensive irrigation well installed. A halver didn't question his landlord. Even though Mr. Lysee added the large cost of the well to their debt.

Once Irving began his soft, quiet snore, Hester snuck out with Reggie to make love amidst the growing cotton. It was a little over a foot high, the first of the cotton squares just beginning to show, little green purses holding the wet bud. The green scent of it, the distant rustling of something living, the moon, bright, casting its cream-colored light on their backs, their hands, their faces. When they were finished, they sat in silence for a while, watching as the night breathed around them. They were not touching—they sat close, side-by-side—but the space in between their bodies was not a separation, but a connection, a silent understanding. She knew this man, and he knew her. They didn't need to be wrapped around each other all the time for the knowing to be there. Hester knew Reggie like she knew the back of her own eyelids. She knew he had something on his mind, and she didn't need to push him; when he had something to say, in his own time, he would speak.

"I need my good shirt sewed up Saturday afternoon," he said.

"The brown one with the ripped shoulder?"

"Mmm."

"Why for?"

"Need it for church Sunday."

Hester waited. Reggie was quiet for a long time.

"Lysee want to see me come Monday," he said.

"What he want you for?"

"Don't know."

Reggie fell silent again.

"I reckon it ain't good."

"How you reckon that?"

"Got a bad feelin. Was walkin over there through the corn, lookin out for earworms, and I seed a dead crow. Then Lysee send his boy to tell me come see him Monday." He spit, leaning away so it'd land where they wouldn't step. "Bad omen."

Hester laughed. "What you doin runnin round scared of a dead bird? Full grown man like you. Mr. Lysee want to see you, all right; he want to tell you he fixin to pay you twenty dollar a bale."

Reggie snickered. "Us be livin mighty good, then," he said.

Hester shifted to face him. "Well, now you got me talkin bout good livin, I been meanin to talk with you bout what we goin to do with Irving."

Reggie nodded. "His schoolin?"

"They just promoted him from the eighth grade—how we goin to find a high school for him?"

"He sho nuff got more schoolin than you or me."

Thanks to Ida, Hester's education was better than most— Reggie could do figures, but he could barely read or write. "I means to see him to college."

"I means it too," Reggie said.

"I got enough put away for high school, I reckon, but not college yet." Though there was nobody around, Hester whispered this out of habit. Her savings were a closely kept secret—not even Irving knew about it. If some stoolpigeon let it leak that she was holding money, any white man could come and take it from her. Mr. Lysee could say they owed it toward their debt (though, somehow, they would still most likely come up short); they could say they owed it in back taxes; they could just take it, and there wasn't a policeman, a lawyer, or a court in Mississippi that would get it back for them.

"How much you got?" Reggie whispered.

"Two hundred and seventeen dollar."

Reggie let out a low whistle. "And that ain't enough for college?"

"I reckon it ain't," she said.

Reggie whistled again.

There was a gentle breeze that made the cotton whisper. "I knowed this day would come," she said. "Since Irving was just a knee-baby I knowed it would."

"What day you mean?"

"The day we got to study how to send Irving away from here. I knowed it would come, but now it here, I ain't ready for it."

"Where we goin to send him to?"

Hester shook her head. "Don't know. Jackson, I reckon."

"To Beth cousin?"

"Mmm. But my launderin done dried up; what we goin send Beth cousin to keep him on?"

"Don't have nothin extra to send."

"She can't keep him on nothin."

Reggie grunted. "What about sendin him out this country?"

"To my sister?"

"Mmm."

It was something they had discussed before, sending Irving to New York with Ida, who lived in a place called Rochester, which was not the same as New York City. There, he'd have plenty of food and a good house to live in, he'd get a far better education than he could get even in Jackson, he'd be free of the constant threat, the great white thumb pressed to the nape of the neck as a reminder that you'd better, and you'd better not, that you ain't and you is, that you fall back or get felled. They'd spoken about this before, and what had always held them back was this: the North was a different country, one that would demand Irving's assimilation. The North would ruin him for the South, so that on the rare occasion Irving made it down to visit his parents—and they would only very rarely get to see him, their son, their only child—he'd be a stranger, an outsider. Against his life in New York, he'd see how shameful their way of living was; he'd pity his own parents, feel ashamed of them. Soon, he'd stop visiting. He'd forget where he came from. They'd lose their son. Hester had seen this play out before.

Reggie also understood all this, Hester knew, felt all this, but as desperate as he was not to lose Irving, he was just as desperate to give him something better. Hester was somewhere in the middle. To hold your children down to keep them near, to hold them down because they needed a good measure of get down in them to survive, was slavery. But to send her only baby upriver knowing she'd hardly ever see him again was also slavery. So, to Reggie, she said, "Ida is on some tough times too, I reckon. She just lost her husband, God rest his soul, and she got four chil'ren of her own to feed. It ain't right sendin another mouth and no money to feed it with."

Reggie shrugged.

Hester made no answer to that and they again sat in quiet for a while. Nothing but the whispering cotton, the distant, hellish blare of a barn owl.

"Why come your father never gathered you all up and left this country? He coulda done it—he knew how to get things from white folks. Why come he never stoled y'all away?"

Hester shook her head. "This was his home," she said. "Sho nuff knowed the South had its troubles when it come to the Negro, and he wanted better for Ida, but his roots go deep in this land, to back before the surrender. Everything that growed on this land, he made it to grow. I think if my mama'd told him she were leavin this country for good, he would-a tole her to be sure and write."

"And what about you?" Reggie asked. "Is your roots caught up in this land?"

"Why, yes, they is," she answered. She looked out over the field, listening to the barn owl's unearthly cry. "But a old plant still grow new roots."

Once again, they fell into silence. In time, they saw the barn owl, flying slowly and silently overhead, hunting; a stark, white shape in the cream moonlight, the sky a dark screen behind it. Reggie grunted and spat again, but Hester couldn't remember whether owls were a good sign or bad.

It was Hester's turn to fry the chicken for the after church meal and she'd burned some of it, letting the oil get too hot over the fire. The white meat inside was still tender and moist, but the skin was burnt. She had almost cried about it. Normally, she was not so touchy about her chicken; normally, she wouldn't have burnt it in the first place. But this was going to be the last after church meal she'd prepare, as far as she knew.

Reggie had been right. Mr. Lysee had not had good news.

Reggie said that Mr. Lysee had met him looking in a bad way—unshaven, eyes red-rimmed, shirt stained, hat askew. Reggie said that it struck him funny, that he'd got his shirt sewed up just to meet Mr. Lysee, and here Lysee come out looking like that. He looked like the Carpenters, the Merrills, the Berricks—white tenants on the nearby Debry plantation. The Merrills and the Berricks were all right; Hester and Ida used to play with Nancy and Jacob and Merrilee a little when they were kids. But those Carpenters were mean, hated black folks, even after that one winter when Hester kept bringing them cornpone, butter beans, and onions because their vegetables never came up and they would've starved otherwise.

Here Mr. Lysee was, looking like one of those poor tenants from around the way, and the first thing he said to Reggie was, I'm mighty sorry about it, boy, truly I am. And Reggie knew right then he'd been right about that dead crow in the corn. That drought done me in, said Mr. Lysee. And my stocks got shot—I can't pay my mortgage. Now, what do you want me to do? He spoke to Reggie like Reggie was putting up an argument, though he hadn't said a word. I have to sell to the bank, I have to. Ain't got a choice. You tell me if you can, just what am I supposed to do different? Still, Reggie said nothing. The bank's got machines, boy, Mr. Lysee said. Plows, tractors, grain drills. They won't need you. I'm mighty sorry about it, boy, but there's nothing I can do. Awfully sorry.

Reggie said that Mr. Lysee truly looked sorry; he even took off his hat at one point, but, remembering himself, quickly put it back on, letting it be just as askew as it was before. Now, said Mr. Lysee, to be truthful, to tell the honest truth, you all owe a big debt. I take all the risk, you understand? Sometimes I've envied you, because I take on all the risk, and you all owe me a large debt. But I'm a good man, a God-fearing man, and on account of all the things your wife and her family done for me and mine, I'm willing to call it settled, right here. All I ask is for you to hand over them chickens, cows, and the hogs. Then I'll call the whole thing settled. And look here: I'm giving you a full month's notice. That's by far more consideration than any other planter woulda given you. I tell you, you find me a planter more sympathetic in all this here country, and I'll be damned right on this spot.

Reggie had naturally agreed to Lysee's terms and oiled the man thoroughly with thanks, and now Hester was trying to think what to do next, and some of the chicken was burnt. But only some of it. And the biscuits—they always asked her to make her mother's famous biscuits—came out fine like they always did. She set the basket of chicken and the basket of biscuits on the big table the men had set up outside.

Lysee's other men got the news too—Jim Thurgood and his family and Maxwell Ames and his family. Jim got Mr. Roland Smith to take over his debt at ninety percent, and Maxwell got Mr. Van Thorpe to do the same. Only Reggie had had his debt cleared, and it was because of the generations Hester's family had spent working his family's land on halves. Longer if he counted the labor put in from slavery. So Reggie didn't name anybody to take up their debt, and in a month, Lysee was going to let them free. Hester had never been free a day in her life, and now that it was coming, she was unprepared, put upon, full of fear and useless anger. They would have nothing but two-hundred and seventeen dollars, a couple of mules, and an old dog to their name.

And Lysee, harangued as Reggie said he looked, must be making a profit somewhere. He must be, or else he wouldn't let their debt go, a debt built on joint notes, on poor crops, on overpriced fertilizer and seed, on seventeen percent interest rates, on crooked mortgages. It fired Hester up. She'd counted Lysee as a good one—never spoke an impolite word to any of them, never forced them to sign anything they couldn't read, never tried to cut in on them on how to live their lives outside of their work. Yes, he overcharged for supplies in his store, set up interest rates on their advances and rations money that kept them in debt, mortgaged their animals and wagons so they couldn't sell them, but Hester had never held any of that against him. That was just how business was done in this country.

But for Lysee to use up all their labor—their tilling, their turning, their cultivating and planting and irrigating and fertilizing—only to drop the fruit into the bank's hands so all the bank had to do was use their fancy machines to pick it, for Lysee to somehow, somewhere be making a fat profit while they got cheated out of their share of the crops they raised, of the pay for their labor, and for Lysee to do this with the idea that he was a good, God-fearing man, that he had done right by Hester and her family—it fired her up. But there was nothing that could be done about that fire but to hold it inside, let it burn up or burn out.

She arranged the burnt pieces of chicken at the bottom of the cloth-lined basket. People were beginning to gather. The men eyed the table hungrily, and other women set out other dishes—cornpone, stewed greens, sweet potatoes, salt pork, sweet beans, freshly made jams and ginger cakes. No one complained about the chicken, and the young men joked, fighting with each other over the last of the biscuits.

Everyone made sure that the children got enough to eat before eating their own fill. Everyone knew what it was like to be hungry as a child. Hester remembered years from her own childhood when all there was to eat was flour bread and a pot of stringy meat, or just milk, eggs, and corn. When the Negro school was open, all there was all day was turnips from the school's turnip patch, and by the time she got home, her stomach would be turning those turnips over and over, cramping her belly. Every adult knew what that was like. So when there was food, unless you were a mean, lawless tough like Calvin Armstrong or Mike Little, you made sure the children got some first. After the eating, there was music. Someone had a guitar, someone else a fifty-cent harmonica, and someone else used the table as a drum. Four young men got up to sing.

Don't you let nobody turn you roun
Don't you let nobody turn you roun
Keep the straight and narrow way

A car drove down the road, and everyone stopped to watch it. A fern green Cadillac with the roof down—Mr. Simon Roussell. He was a very wealthy planter from Louisiana; dealt in cane, but he lived part of the year in Coahoma. Through his late wife, he had some land nearby—Justice Shaw grew his cotton for him. Hester and everyone else stood up straight, ready to wave as he passed. But as he drove closer, Hester got a look at his passenger—a young-looking man, a stranger. As discreetly as they could, mothers beckoned their children to their sides, and men idled closer to their wives. The razor-eyed wariness of a prey animal. Reggie came to stand ever so slightly in front of Hester and Irving.

Mr. Roussell stopped his car in front of the church, and he and the young, pale man got out of the car. People who had been peacefully eating around the side of the church put down their food and came around to the front, where Mr. Roussell could see them and they could see him. Nobody spoke. Nobody looked around at each other. No one looked directly at Mr. Roussell or his guest, but looked around them—over their shoulders, at their hands. They were all one living thing now; instinctually, they had merged into one cagey animal, with Pastor Holmes as its suspicious, deer-eyed head.

Pastor Holmes stepped forward, grinning the grin white men liked: wide, lots of teeth, eyes dull and mischievous as a child's. "Afternoon, Mr. Roussell," he said. "And blessins to you on a fine Sunday."

"What were you darkies doing here? Looked like you had you some music."

Roussell was a man who never called a Negro a *nigger*, but *nigger* was what he meant. He'd smile and say *darky* or *spook*, but you knew he just meant *nigger*.

"Why, we sho nuff was celebratin the Lord with a little singin, we was, Mr. Roussell, and Mr. ..."

"This here's Mr. Ashbury, my new son-in-law."

"Pleasured to meet your acquaintanceship, Suh," Pastor Holmes said with a bow.

"He's from Connecticut. A real carpetbagger." Roussell meant it in good humor. Both he and Mr. Ashbury chuckled. Mr. Ashbury was so pale—Hester wondered if he was sick.

Pastor Holmes made no response but kept grinning.

"Thought I'd take him for a nice drive through the country," Roussell said.

"A mighty welcome to you, Suh," Pastor Holmes said.

Mr. Ashbury looked like he might faint.

"Say," said Roussell, "how bout letting Mr. Ashbury hear some of that good ole spade music? I do reckon he hasn't heard it before."

Pastor Holmes grinned at the two white men some more and looked over his shoulder at the four who had been singing before. They adjusted their collars and stepped forward, looking at each other from the sides of their eyes, communicating silently before setting their voices loose on a slow, austere melody.

You may bury me in de East
You may bury me in de West
But I'll hear de trumpet sound in a-dat mornin
In a-dat mornin, my Lawd
How I long to go
For to hear de trumpet sound in a-dat mornin

When they finished their song, they kept their heads bowed, kept looking at each other from the sides of their eyes. One of them lightly kicked at the dirt with the tip of his Sunday shoe.

"Lovely," Mr. Ashbury nearly whispered. Hester tried not to stare at the bright red blotches that appeared on his cheeks, bursts of red valerian blossoms.

"Oh, come now," said Roussell, "sing us something lively. Something with that good ole darky zip to it. And can't none of these here pickaninnies dance a little?"

Again, Pastor Holmes grinned, and again the singers looked at each other out the sides of their eyes. Pastor Holmes looked over his shoulder, still grinning, and nodded at Tirzah. With only a hint of hesitation, she pushed forward Tobiah, Abraham, and Jacob. The men with the guitar and the harmonica gathered up their instruments and stepped forward, and the man who had been drumming at the table resumed his position.

Live a-humble

                    Humble

Humble yo'self, de bell done ring
Glory and honor

                    Praise King Jesus

Glory and honor

                    Praise de Lawd

Tirzah's boys shuffled their feet around in the dirt, moving their hips this way, grinning here, clapping there. Jacob was only seven, and so he shuffled along clumsily, not quite to the rhythm, looking up to copy his older brothers. Others in the crowd began to clap, nod their heads, stomp their feet. But it wasn't for the two white men watching. It was for themselves, for the young singers, for the dancing children.

> *God's gwinter call dem chil'ren from a distant land*
> *Tombstones a-crackin, graves a-bustin*
> *Hell an de sea am gwinter give up de dead*
> *False pretender wear sheep clothin on his back*
> *In his heart he like a ravin wolf*
> > *Judge ye not, brother*

Hester resisted the urge to grab Irving and pull him against her. He was nobody's trained monkey. She watched the red valerian bloom on Mr. Ashbury's cheeks. She wondered what white people did after church on Sundays, that they had time to drive out into the country looking for a minstrel show.

> *Watch the sun how steady he run*
> *Dun let him catch you wid yo work undone*
> *Glory and honor*
> > *Praise King Jesus*
> *Glory and honor*
> > *Praise de Lawd*

This time, Roussell hooted and took off his hat, waving it around in the air before setting it back on his head again. The singers did not move, holding their straw hats in their hands. The children scurried back to their mother. "Ain't that fine," said Roussell. "Ain't that just fine."

Mr. Ashbury made no answer, and Pastor Holmes only kept up that glossy grin.

"But can't you sing one of them blues songs?" Roussell said. "A nice blues song with some vim to it."

"Now, Mr. Roussell," Pastor Holmes said, a hint of edge to his voice. "It *is* a Sunday."

"Right you are, right you are," Roussell chuckled. He reached into his jacket pocket and pulled out a dollar each for the young singers. To each of the musicians, he gave a quarter. And he gave a penny to Tirzah.

"That's mighty gen'rous of you, Suh," said Pastor Holmes.

"You been tellin these folks how the Lord smile upon a hard day's work?" Roussell said.

"Yes, Suh," said Pastor.

"Exceptin on a Sunday, of course."

"Of course, Suh."

"I don't let my boys work on a Sunday. I never let em."

"No, Suh. Mighty gen'rous."

"You hear that, Ashbury? Never let your darkies work on a Sunday. Spoils em for any other day's work."

Mr. Ashbury nodded, his head like a heavy boll bobbing on its stem.

Roussell adjusted his jacket around his shoulders, rocked briefly onto the balls of his feet and back again, sniffed. "Well, Holmes," he said, "I think we'll be on our way."

"Yes, Suh," Pastor Holmes said. "May the Lord bless you, Suh."

"You all be good," Roussell said, looking over all of them. Mr. Ashbury was already halfway to the Cadillac when Roussell's eyes fell on Hester. "Ah—Auntie Hester."

Hester stiffened. She nodded at Roussell. "Afternoon Mr. Roussell, Mr. Ashbury."

"I remember your sister. How is she doin with that fine education?"

There was the subtle gleam of nastiness behind Roussell's words.

"She not doin too good at all, Mr. Roussell. Her husband passed, Suh."

Roussell gave her the condescendingly sympathetic look one gave a child crying over dropped candy. "What a shame," he said. "A shame, a shame."

"Yes, Suh," said Hester.

"Yes, I'm awfully sorry to hear that."

"Thank you, Suh."

"But, Auntie Hester—I recall your sister having a lovely white smile. And here you are, looking awfully somber on a

Sunday. Can't you spare us a nice, white smile?"

As her face arranged itself into the smile Roussell wanted, the cute, white, mammy smile, Hester felt rather than saw Reggie flow closer to her, just barely touching her hand with the back of his. "I sho nuff can smile under the Lord's eye," she said.

"Glad to hear it, Auntie. All right, give Auntie Ida my regards, my *devoirs*—that's a good, educated word for her. I'm sure she'll find herself another husband in no time."

"Yes, Suh. I will, Suh."

This satisfied Roussell, and he spun on his heel and returned to his car. Mr. Ashbury was already inside, thin and tall like cotton gone to weed, pale with those valerian splotches on his cheeks. Roussell and his young son-in-law drove off in the fern green Cadillac, and the dirt road rose up and grabbed at the back of that car as it left. No one stayed for long after that.

———

NICOLE CUFFY is a New York based writer with a BA from Columbia University and an MFA from the New School. When she is not writing, she is reading, and when she is not reading, she is doing yoga. She can be found muddling her way through Twitter at @nicolethecuffy.

CPSIA information can be obtained
at www.ICGtesting.com
Printed in the USA
FFOW05n0147271017